Michiko Aoyama was born in 1970 in Aichi Prefecture, Japan. After graduating from university, she worked for two years as a reporter for a Japanese newspaper based in Sydney before moving back to Japan to work as a magazine editor for a publishing company in Tokyo. Her debut novel, *Cocoa on Thursday*, won the inaugural Miyazaki Book Award. A later work, *The Cat's Tale under the Tree*, won the Tenryu Literature Prize. Her other works include *Kamakura Uzumaki Information Centre*, *God Is On Duty Now*, *Monday Matcha Café*, *My Present*, *Usual Thursday*, *In the Moon Forest*, and *Red, Blue and Esquisse*. *What You Are Looking For Is in the Library* was short-listed for the Japan Booksellers' Award and became a Japanese bestseller. It is being translated into more than twenty languages. She lives in Yokohama, Japan.

Alison Watts has translated *The Boy and the Dog* by Seishu Hase and *Sweet Bean Paste* by Durian Sukegawa, in addition to novels by Naoki Matayoshi and Riku Onda.

What you are looking for is in the library

A Novel

Michiko Aoyama

Translated from the Japanese by Alison Watts

HANOVER
SQUARE
PRESS

HANOVER
SQUARE
PRESS™

Recycling programs
for this product may
not exist in your area.

ISBN-13: 978-1-335-00562-5

What You Are Looking For Is in the Library

Copyright © 2020 by Michiko Aoyama

First English-language edition published in Great Britain in 2023 by Doubleday, an imprint of Transworld Publishers. This edition published in 2023.

Originally published in Japan in 2020 as お探し物は図書室まで by POPLAR Publishing Co., Ltd.

Translation from the Japanese copyright © 2023 by Alison Watts

English language translation rights arranged with POPLAR Publishing Co., Ltd.

Internal illustrations copyright © 2023 by Rohan Eason

Hanover Square Press
22 Adelaide St. West, 41st Floor
Toronto, Ontario M5H 4E3, Canada
HanoverSqPress.com
BookClubbish.com

Printed in U.S.A.

1

Tomoka, 21, womenswear sales assistant

When Saya sends a text to tell me she has a new boy-friend, I instantly write back: What's he like? But all she replies is: He's a doctor. Nothing about looks or personality, or what kind of doctor he is—I mean, he could be any kind, couldn't he? It's true I know what she means by *doctor*. Jobs can be a clue to somebody's character. A short-cut way of describing them. But only in a limited, stereotyped sort of way.

That starts me thinking: what do people think about me based on my job? What does it say about my personality or qualities?

I've known Saya since high school. She's a friend from back home who's kept in touch ever since I left to come to college in Tokyo. She sends me texts every now and then. Bit by bit, the story of how she met her new boy-friend at a party appears on the pale sky-blue screen of my smartphone. Then she writes: How r u doing?

With my finger poised above the screen, I tap *b* and *brilliant* pops up in the auto-predict, so I just select it and tap send. What I really meant to say, though, was *bored*.

~

I work at Eden. That sounds like paradise, doesn't it, but it's actually a chain of general merchandise stores, not as upmarket as a department store. Every morning I put on my tight black skirt and matching waistcoat to go and spend the day serving customers and working behind the till. I started this job six months ago after graduating from junior college. The time has flown by. I started in spring and now it's nearly winter. In November, when the heating was turned on in the store, my feet started getting sweaty inside in my stockings, mak-ing my toes squish together and bunch up in my tight pumps. Most women who have to wear a uniform at work probably feel the same. The thing that makes the Eden uniform special, though, are the blouses. They're a kind of peachy-orange color called coral pink, which was selected by a famous color coordinator. We learned that during training. Coral pink supposedly projects a bright, caring image, and is flattering to women of all ages. I saw the coordinator's point when I started work in my assigned section of Womenswear.

~

"Miss Fujiki, I've had my break. You can go next."

That's Mrs. Numauchi, one of the part-time workers.

When she returns to the counter, her lips look shiny and moist. Obviously retouched. Mrs. Numauchi is an old hand who's been working here the last twelve years. Last month when it was her birthday she said that she'd reached a number with two digits the same. She can't be forty-four or sixty-six, so I guess she's fifty-five. Around my mother's age.

Like I said, I really get it about the coral pink—it looks good on Mrs. Numauchi, too. That color coordinator must've been aware that most of the staff here are part-time older women.

"Miss Fujiki, you've been cutting it close coming back from your break recently. You should be more punctual."

"I'm sorry."

Mrs. Numauchi is really bossy. She's so picky about trivial things, and sometimes acts like she's in charge, but she's usually right, so I put up with it.

"Okay, I'm going," I say and bow to take my leave.

While walking across the shop floor, I stop to straighten some clothes that I happen to notice are out of place.

"Ah, excuse me," a customer calls.

I turn around to see a lady in a frumpy old down jacket with a frayed backpack. Even though she must be as old as Mrs. Numauchi, she doesn't have any makeup on.

"Which one do you like best?" she asks, and holds up two knitted tops in turn: a mulberry V-neck followed by a light-brown turtleneck.

In Womenswear we don't make a point of approaching customers as the staff at in-store boutiques do. I'm really glad of that, but if a customer asks for help, then of course I have to assist.

"Let me see…" I say, looking at each one to compare them, secretly wishing I'd ignored the untidy shelf and gone straight out on my break. I point to the mulberry top. "This one's nice, don't you think? Very elegant."

"Do you think so? It's not too flamboyant for me?"

"No, not at all. But if you're looking for something less conspicuous, the brown one would be nice and warm around the neck."

"But I think it might be a bit drab."

And so on and so on. The pointless exchange drags on. I ask if she'd like to try the tops on but, no, that's too much trouble. I have to stop myself from sighing.

Touching the mulberry top I say to her, "This is a lovely color and it really suits you, I think."

"You do?" The customer stares at it for a long time then looks up.

At last…is she going to make up her mind?

"Well, I suppose I'll take it," she says, and goes off to pay for it at the till.

Hooray! I fold the brown turtleneck and return it to the shelf. There goes fifteen minutes of my precious break down the drain.

As I'm heading through the staff exit at the rear, one of the girls from a brand boutique on the same floor brushes past me. She's wearing a gorgeous moss-green and white country-style check skirt that flares out and swings as she walks. She has her hair up in a cute bun to complete the look. I wonder if her clothes are from the boutique. Uniforms aren't compulsory for boutique staff; they can wear their own clothes. Having girls like that around makes even Eden feel a bit more of a cool place.

I collect the vinyl tote bag with my lunch things in it from the locker room, then head for the staff canteen. It has a pretty limited lunch menu: soba or udon noodles, curry or a weekly special set lunch that always has something deep-fried. I ordered lunch from the canteen a few times, but then I got my head bitten off once by the woman in the kitchen when I told her she'd made

11

a mistake with my order. So now I buy a sandwich or savory roll at a convenience store on the way to work.

Women's blouses dot the room in splashes of pink, among the men in their white shirts and boutique staff in casual dress. Four women part-timers at a table near me are having fun chatting and laughing noisily about their husbands and children. To a customer I would look like one of them in my coral-pink blouse. But to be honest, those ladies scare me. I can't stand up to them, and try not to get into any kind of exchange with them.

There is one reason and one reason only that I work at Eden: it was the only job offer I received. I didn't put much thought into my application. It was just one out of many that I sent off at the end of junior college. I didn't think there was much I was capable of doing anyway, so anywhere that was willing to take me was fine with me. I'd received about thirty rejections and was totally fed up by the time the offer from Eden arrived, so I accepted it immediately. Besides, it ticked the most important box for me—it was in Tokyo. But it wasn't that I wanted to live there so much as I didn't want to go back to the country.

Where I come from is a long, long way from Tokyo. A place with rice fields, rice fields and more rice fields, in every direction as far as the eye can see. The nearest convenience store is a fifteen-minute drive, and even that is just one lonely shop all by itself on a main road. Magazines always go on sale a few days later than anywhere else. There are no cinemas or fashion stores. Nothing you could call a restaurant, either; the closest thing to eating out are the small local diners with set menus. I'd been dying of boredom there ever since I was a teenager, and couldn't wait to get away at the first opportunity.

I had an image of Tokyo from the dramas I used to watch on the four limited TV stations that were available to us. Tokyo was the ultimate, the dream city that had everything. If I could only make it there, my life, too, would be as cool and fun as the lives of the actresses I saw on TV. At least that's what I believed. It was also what drove me to study hard at high school, so I could get into junior college in Tokyo.

Once I made it here, however, I realized what a fantasy world I'd been living in. Tokyo is still a dream, though—I mean, there is always at least one convenience store within five minutes' walk, and the trains come every three minutes! Plus anything you could possibly want in the way of daily necessities and ready-prepared food is available at your fingertips, at any time. After I'd been accepted for training with Eden, I was assigned to a store just one train stop away from where I was already living.

Sometimes, though, I think about the future. What

will I be doing years from now? I don't have the same kind of burning desire like I used to when all I wanted was to escape to Tokyo, and I don't feel excited any more about achieving a goal. That all fizzled away, like froth.

Hardly anyone in my hometown goes to college in Tokyo, so having people tell me how amazing I was used to make me feel good, but when it comes down to it I'm not amazing at all. I have no ambitions, nothing I enjoy—I don't even have a boyfriend. It's hard to see anyone since I don't have weekends off. I know there's more to it than that, but I still can't find a guy.

The only reason I don't go back home is because I couldn't stand putting up with the inconvenience of country life again.

What will I do? I worry about the years slipping by, while I stay on at Eden getting older and older. Living a life with no dreams or ambitions, getting old and wrinkled inside my coral-pink blouse.

Find a new job, Tomoka. This thought has been on my mind a lot recently. But it feels such a huge effort to do anything about it. Basically I'm not very driven. Even writing a CV is a big hassle for me. Anyway, what else can a girl like me do? A young recent junior college graduate with no skills, who only Eden was willing to employ.

~

"Hey, Tomoka," calls Kiriyama. He works behind the counter at the in-store branch of ZAZ, a chain selling eyeglasses. He's twenty-five, four years older than me, and the only person at Eden I can really talk to—his eyes are friendly. He started working here four months ago but I haven't seen him in a while. Because he's an employee of ZAZ, not Eden, he sometimes he gets called to help at other ZAZ branches.

Kiriyama is holding a tray loaded with a deep-fried mackerel set lunch and a bowl of udon noodles topped with meat. For someone so thin, he really eats a lot.

"Okay if I join you?"

"Sure," I tell him, and he sits down opposite me. He wears thin-framed round glasses that really suit him. You can tell he's doing exactly what he should be doing. Though I remember hearing that he did other work before ZAZ.

"Kiriyama, what did you used to do?" I ask.

"Do—me? Ah, print production. Magazines, that kind of thing. Editing, writing, stuff like that."

"Really? Wow." I didn't know he worked in publishing. All of a sudden my impression of him switches from gentle-mannered, nice guy to smart intellectual. See, even previous jobs have the power to influence your image of a person.

"Why so surprised?"

"But you had an amazing job."

Kiriyama smiles and slurps down his noodles. "Working in a glasses shop is also amazing."

"Oh, sure, yeah." I smile, too, and take a bite of my sausage bread.

"'Amazing' is your favorite word, isn't it, Tomoka?"

"Um, maybe."

He might be right, though. When Saya was telling me about her boyfriend, I might've used the word "amazing" more than a few times. What do I think is amazing, I wonder. A special talent? A deep knowledge of something? A unique skill?

"I'm gonna end up in Eden for the rest of my life," I whisper into my strawberry milk.

"What's up? Do you want to change jobs?"

"Yeah…" I say after a pause. "I've been thinking about it lately."

"Do you still want to work in customer service?"

"Yeah. But I wouldn't mind working in an office. So I can have weekends off, and wear whatever I like, and have my own desk. I could go to a café near work for lunch with my colleagues, and bitch about the boss in the tearoom…"

"I don't hear anything about the actual job in any of those scenarios," says Kiriyama.

That can't be helped. I mean, I don't even know myself what kind of job I want to do.

"But you're a permanent, Tomoka. In a few years you can transfer to head office, can't you?"

"I guess so, but…"

After starting with the company, permanent staff have to put in three years at a branch store. Once you have the sales experience, you can apply for a transfer to head office. You can try for General Affairs, or Human Resources, or Product Development and become a buyer or an event planner. Any of these would suit me. But I'd also heard that in reality the chances of a transfer application being approved were low. The most realistic outcome was rising to division chief, like my uninspiring boss.

Mr. Ueshima is thirty-five and has been in the same position for the last five years. When I look at him, I get the feeling that this is all I can ever hope for, even if things go well. Sure, I might get a promotion, but the work would be the same. The only thing that'd be different is having more responsibility, supervising the part-time staff mainly. Just the thought of it gives me the heebie-jeebies. The pay might be a bit better but I really don't feel I could pull it off.

"How'd you find the job at ZAZ?" I ask Kiriyama.

"I registered on a career-change site and got a good response. So I chose from the offers."

He pulls out his smartphone to show me the site. You select the descriptions matching the kind of work you're looking for, give details of your experience and skills, and wait for emails with matching offers. The information required seems to be quite specific. Qualifications, TOEIC scores, driving license… Just tick the boxes.

"But I don't have any skills. Only Level 3 for the English proficiency test."

I wish I at least had my driving license. Back home, everybody used to register for driving lessons in the spring vacation immediately after finishing high school, because that's the kind of place it is. You can't do anything if you don't drive. But I was going off to college in Tokyo, so I didn't think I needed to and instead I spent my last vacation mucking about. While scanning the site registration form, I notice that computer skills are listed: Word, Excel, Powerpoint… Plus others I've never even heard of.

I do at least own a laptop. I used it at college for writing reports and my graduation thesis. But once I started working I didn't need to write that kind of thing anymore, so when my router broke I couldn't be bothered

buying another one or getting it connected it to Wi-Fi—
mainly because I didn't know how to—and I haven't
used it since. Almost everything I need to do I can do
on my smartphone.

"I can use Word, I guess, but not Excel."

"If you want to work in an office, you have to know
Excel."

"Computer courses are expensive, though."

"You don't have to go on computer courses," Kiriyama tells me. "Community centers often have that kind
of thing. Cheap classes for local residents."

"What—really? I didn't know that," I say, looking
down at the time on my wristwatch while I fold up the
plastic wrappers from my lunch. Only ten minutes of
break left—I should get back to the till three minutes
before time or Mrs. Numauchi will be on my case again,
but I need to go to the toilet first. Draining the last of
my strawberry milk in one gulp, I stand up and leave.

∼

Later that evening, I tap out *Hatori*—the name of the
ward where I live—*ward resident* and *computer class* on
my smartphone. And wow, I can't believe the number
of hits. Who would've thought there was so much out

there! My eyes rest on a link that says *Hatori Community House*. It seems to be connected to an elementary school less than ten minutes' walk from my apartment.

I click for more information. This place has all kinds of classes and events: shogi, haiku, eurhythmics, hula dancing, exercise classes, *lots* of flower-arranging classes and lectures on different topics. I've never heard of an elementary school doing this kind of thing, let alone one I've lived near for the last three years.

The computer class costs 2,000 yen a time and is held every Wednesday from two to four, which is great for me. Especially as this coming Wednesday happens to be my rostered day off.

Students can take their own laptop or borrow one at the class. Lessons are customized but it's not a course and you can attend whenever you want. I read the teacher's introductory message:

Beginners welcome. Study at your own pace with individual guidance. Instruction in basic computer skills, Word, Excel, building a website and programming.
Y. Gonno

Already I can see myself using Excel like a pro, and for the first time in a long while, I feel slightly excited about something.

~

Two days later, I'm standing outside the elementary school with my laptop in hand. I follow the directions from the Community House home page and walk along the school fence until I reach a narrow road. There it is: a two-story white building with a sign over the canopy at the entrance that says "Hatori Community House."

I go through a glass door and see an old guy with bushy gray hair at the front desk. In the office behind him, a woman with a bandana sits at a desk writing something.

"Um, I'm here for the computer class," I say to the old guy.

"Put your name down here. It's in Meeting Room A." He points at a folder on the countertop. A sheet of paper inside has a table with columns headed *Name*, *Purpose of visit*, *Time of arrival* and *Time of departure*.

Meeting Room A is on the ground floor. Going past the front desk to the lobby, I turn right and find it immediately. Through an open sliding door I can see two students sitting at long tables facing each other with their laptops open: a girl a bit older than me with soft wavy hair and an old guy with a square face.

The teacher turns out to be a woman, not a man. Ms. Gonno is probably in her fifties.

I go over and introduce myself. "Hello, my name is Tomoka Fujiki."

She gives me a friendly smile. "Please, sit wherever you like."

I choose to sit at the same table as the girl, but at the other end. She and the old guy are concentrating so hard on their own stuff they take no notice of me. I open up my laptop, which I'd already started up at home since I haven't used it in ages and which took forever to boot. My fingers feel like bananas on the keyboard, probably because I only ever use a smartphone. I should probably do some practice in Word as well.

"Ms. Fujiki, you want to learn Excel, don't you?" says Ms. Gonno, glancing down at my computer.

"Yes. But this computer doesn't have Excel."

She looks at my screen again and moves the mouse around a bit. "Yes it does. I'll make a shortcut for you."

A green icon with an X for Excel appears at the edge of the screen. No way! Excel has been hiding in my computer all along?

"I can see you've used Word, so I assume you have Office installed."

I don't have a clue what she's talking about... But I did ask a friend at college to set up Word for me when I couldn't figure it out for myself. Maybe that's how it got in there. This is what happens when you leave stuff up to other people.

For the next two hours, I learn all about Excel. Ms. Gonno wanders between me and the other two but I get special attention, because I'm the newcomer, I suppose.

The most amazing thing I learn is how to perform addition by highlighting cells. Just press a key and *bam!* with one touch they all add up! It impresses me so much I can't help cheering, which Ms. Gonno seems to find funny.

While practising as instructed, I overhear the conversation between Ms. Gonno and the other students. I get the impression they are regulars: the old guy is building a website about wildflowers, while the girl is setting up an online shop. I feel like such a waster. All the time I've been lazing around in my apartment doing nothing, not far away these two have been getting on with stuff—learning things! The more I think about it, the more pathetic it makes me feel.

When it's nearly time to finish, Ms. Gonno says, "There's no set textbook, but I'll give you a list of recommended titles. Don't restrict yourself to these, though. Have a browse in a library or bookshop and see what you can find for yourself that's easy to follow." She holds up a computer guide and smiles. "You might like to look in the library here in Community House."

Library. What a nice-sounding word. So comforting.

I feel like I'm a student again. *Library...* "Am I allowed to borrow books?"

"Yes, anybody who lives in the ward can borrow up to six books for two weeks. I think that's the rule."

Then the old guy calls for help and Ms. Gonno goes over to him. I make a note of the recommended titles and leave.

~

The library is also on the ground floor. I pass two meeting rooms and a Japanese-style room at the back of the building beside a small kitchen. The door is wide open with a sign on the wall that says "Library." Rows and rows of bookshelves fill an area about the size of a classroom. A counter to the left of the entrance is marked "Checkouts and Returns." Near the front counter a petite girl in a dark-blue apron is arranging paperbacks on a shelf.

Feeling shy, I approach her. "Excuse me, where are the books on computers?"

Her head jerks up and she blushes. She has huge eyes and hair tied back in a ponytail that swings behind her. She looks young enough to still be at high school. Her name tag says "Nozomi Morinaga."

"Over here." Still holding several paperbacks, Nozomi Morinaga walks past a reading table and guides me to a

large shelf against the wall. "If you need any recommendations, the librarian is in the reference corner."

"Recommendations?"

"You tell her what you're looking for, then she will
do a search and give you recommendations."

I can't find any of the books Ms. Gonno recommended on the shelf. Maybe I should consult the librarian. Nozomi said she was at the back, so I make my
way to the front desk, then look toward the rear. That's
when I notice a screen partition with a sign hanging
from the ceiling that says "Reference."

Heading over, I poke my head around the corner,
and yikes! My eyes nearly jump out of their sockets.
The librarian is huge... I mean, like, really huge. But
huge as in big, not fat. She takes up the entire space between the L-shaped counter and the partition. Her skin
is super pale—you can't even see where her chin ends
and her neck begins—and she is wearing a beige apron
over an off-white, loose-knit cardigan. She reminds me
of a polar bear curled up in a cave for winter. Her hair
is twisted into a small bun right on top of her head, and
she has a cool *kanzashi* hairpin spiked through her bun
with three white flower tassels hanging from it. She is
looking down at something, but I can't see what exactly.
The name tag around her neck says "Sayuri Komachi."
Cute name.

I edge a bit closer and clear my throat. Ms. Komachi's eyes roll up to look at me, without moving any other part of her body. The whites of her eyes are enormous. She's stabbing a needle at something the size of a Ping-Pong ball balanced on a mat the size of a handkerchief. *What* is she doing? Putting a jinx on someone? I almost scream out loud.

"Ah…it's, ah…it's okay," I manage to squeak, but all I want to do is turn tail and get away as fast as possible.

"What are you looking for?"

Her voice…it's so weird… It nails my feet to the floor. As if it has physically grabbed hold of me somehow. But there's a warmth in it that wraps itself around me, making me feel safe and secure, even when it comes from that unsmiling face.

What am I looking for? I'm looking for… A reason to work, something I'm good at—stuff like that. But I don't think that's the kind of answer she expects. "Um, I'm looking for books on how to use a computer."

Ms. Komachi pulls a dark-orange box closer. I recognize the design of white flowers in a hexagon shape. It's a box of Honeydome cookies. I love these. They're dome-shaped, with a soft center, and made by Kuremi-yado, a company that specializes in Western-style confectionery. They're not exactly gourmet, but just a little bit special and not something you can just pick up in a convenience store.

When she lifts the lid, I see a small pair of scissors and some needles. She must be using an empty box for her sewing things. Ms. Komachi puts away her needle and ball, then stares at me.

"What do you want to do on the computer?"

"Excel, to begin with. Enough to tick the boxes on a skills checklist."

"Skills checklist," Ms. Komachi repeats.

"I'm thinking I might register on a career-change site. I'm not that happy with my current job."

"What do you do?"

"Nothing great. Just selling ladies clothes in a general department store."

Ms. Komachi's head tilts to one side. The flower tassels on her hairpin shake and sparkle.

"Is being a sales assistant in a department store really not such a great job?"

I don't know what to say. Ms. Komachi waits patiently for my reply.

"Well, I mean… Anybody can do it. It's not like it was my dream job or anything I desperately wanted to do. I just kind of fell into it. But I live on my own, so I have to work to support myself."

"You managed to find employment, you go to work

every day and you can feed yourself. That's a fine achievement."

Nobody's ever summed up my life in this way before. Her answer makes me want to cry. It's as if she sees me, just as I am.

"But all I do to feed myself is buy stuff from the convenience store," I blurt out clumsily, though I know that's not what she really means by "feed yourself."

Ms. Komachi's head tilts to the other side. "Well, the motive doesn't matter so much as wanting to learn something new. That's a good attitude to have."

She turns to the computer, places both hands on the keyboard and pauses. Then she begins typing, at amazing speed! *Shoo-tatatatata!* Her fingers move in a blur and I nearly fall over myself in surprise.

Ta! She gives one final tap, then delicately lifts her wrists from the keyboard. Next moment, the printer springs into action.

"These should be suitable for a beginner on Excel." Ms. Komachi hands me the sheet. *A Step-by-Step Guide to Word and Excel*, *Excel for Beginners*, *Excel: Fast Efficient Notebooks*, *A Simple Introduction to Office*. Then I notice, right at the bottom, a title that stands out.

Guri and Gura? I stare at the words. The kids' picture book about two field mice, Guri and Gura?

"Oh, and this too." Ms. Komachi swivels on her chair

slightly as she reaches below the counter. I lean forward a bit more to sneak a look and see a wooden cabinet with five drawers. She opens the top one, which seems to be stuffed with soft, colorful objects, picks one out and hands it to me. "Here you are—this is for you."

Automatically I hold out my palm and Ms. Komachi drops a lightweight object on to it. It is round and black, about the size of a large watch face and with a straight bit poking out. *A frying pan?*

The object in my hand is a felted frying pan with a tiny round clasp on the handle.

"Um, what's this?"

"A bonus gift."

"Bonus gift?"

"Yes, something fun, to go with the books."

I stare at the frying pan…er, bonus gift. It is sort of cute.

Ms. Komachi opens the Honeydome box and takes out her needle and ball again. "Have you ever tried felting?"

"No. I've seen it on Twitter and stuff, though."

She holds up her needle for me to see. The top is bent at a right angle for holding it, while the tip at the end has several tiny hooks sticking out.

"Felting is mysterious," she says. "All you do is keep poking the needle at a ball of wool and it turns into a three-dimensional shape. You might *think* that you are simply poking randomly, and the strands are all tangled

29

together, but there is a shape within that the needle will reveal." She jabs roughly at the ball again.

There has to be a ton of felted things inside that drawer. Are they all bonus gifts to give away? But her attention is now completely focused on her hands, as if to say *My job here as librarian is done.*

When I return to the shelf of computer books, I find the recommended titles and choose two that seem easy enough to understand. But what about *Guri and Gura*? Maybe I should get that too. I read it many times when I was in kindergarten. I think I remember my mother reading it to me too. Why would Ms. Komachi recommend this book? Did she make a mistake?

The children's picture books are in a space next to the window sectioned off by low bookshelves. It's a shoes-off area covered with interlocking rubber floor mat tiles. When I enter and find myself surrounded by lots of cute picture books, I feel peaceful all of a sudden. Calmer, and more relaxed. There are three copies of *Guri and Gura*. I guess the library keeps multiple copies because it's such a classic. Maybe I will borrow it... I mean, it's free, isn't it?

So I take my two computer books and *Guri and Gura* over to Nozomi at the checkout counter, show my health-insurance card as ID to apply for a borrower's card, and check out the books.

~

On the way home, I stop at a convenience store and pick up a cinnamon roll and an iced latte. I consume these in front of the TV, but then I feel like something salty and get out some Cup Noodle instant ramen from my stock in the cupboard. By now it's already six o'clock. This will do me for dinner. I fill the kettle and put it on to boil, then get out my new library books to look at while I wait.

I flick through the computer guides, imagining myself already knowing everything inside them and masterfully operating a computer in an office.

Then I take a look at *Guri and Gura*. It has a durable, hard white cover. Somehow I thought it would be bigger. This is hardly any different to a B5-sized notebook. Perhaps it only seemed big to me earlier because of the long pages that open out sideways. The lettering on the cover looks handwritten. Two field mice look at each other across the big basket they are carrying between them. They have matching clothes, one mouse dressed in blue and the other in red. Which is Guri and which is Gura? I'm pretty sure they're twins. I study the cover, and notice that *Guri* in the title is blue and *Gura* is red. Aha!

This discovery gives me a small thrill. Now I have the key, the book is easy to dive into. I flip the pages and follow the story from the pictures. Guri and Gura go into the woods. Oh yeah, that's right, they find a big egg... Toward the end is a picture of a big frying pan with a freshly cooked cake rising up from it. The picture takes up two pages, with the spine cutting through the middle.

This reminds me—didn't Ms. Komachi give me a felt frying pan? I read the text: "The yellow castella showed its soft spongy face."

What? They made castella? I'd been thinking all along it was hotcake. I turn back the page. Egg and sugar, milk and flour. They mix it all up and cook it in the frying pan... Hmm, I didn't know castella was this easy to make.

The kettle begins to whistle. I turn off the gas and peel back the lid of the ramen.

How could I have forgotten the story when I'd read it so many times before? Or misremembered, more like. It's fun, though, to reread a book I loved as a kid. You pick up new things.

I fill the foam cup with boiling water and, just as I'm putting on the lid, my phone rings. Saya's name appears on the screen. Wow, this is unusual. She doesn't normally ring me. Either she's insanely happy, or insanely depressed. I wonder which... For three seconds I hesitate as I glance over at the cup of hot noodles, then I answer.

"Hey, Tomoka, sorry to call out of the blue. Today's your day off, isn't it?"

"Yeah."

"I wanted to ask your advice about something. Is now a good time?"

Saya sounds really apologetic.

"It's fine—what's up?" I ask.

Saya's voice instantly relaxes. "It's Christmas next month, right?" she begins. "So my boyfriend and I decided to tell each other what we want, but I don't know what to ask for. It wouldn't look good to ask for something really expensive, but if it's too cheap, he might be disappointed. You've got a good feel for these things, so I wondered if you had any ideas."

She's happy...

I think of my ramen going soggy if I don't eat them straight away, and regret answering the phone. Just a bit. If this is all she wants to talk about, I could've asked her to wait until after I'd finished eating. But it's too late to say anything now, so I murmur, "Ah," put the phone on speaker mode and place it on the low table. I split the disposable chopsticks in two and eat my ramen as I listen to Saya, trying not to make any noise and saying the right words every now and then to show I am paying attention.

She must have picked up on my lack of enthusiasm from my voice. "Hey, are you busy? What were you doing?" she asks.

I was going to eat my cup ramen. Or rather, I am already eating them, but I don't want her to know this, so I answer, "Hey, it's fine. I was just looking at a picture book. *Guri and Gura*."

"*Guri and Gura*? The story about making a fried egg?"

Woo-hoo, one to me! Hotcake is much closer than a fried egg. "It wasn't a fried egg, you know, it was castella."

"Huh? Really? But it's the story about mice walking through the woods who come across a huge egg, isn't it?"

"That's the one, but the mice talk about what to do with the egg and end up making castella."

"Castella? No way. Only somebody who cooks a lot would think of that. If you don't know what to do with an egg in the first place, you wouldn't think of it."

That's one way of looking at it. I gulp down the remainder of my ramen soup.

Saya keeps talking. "I always knew you were different, Tomoka. I mean to say, reading picture books on your day off—that's really cool. Like, so intellectual. Does everyone in Tokyo do that?"

"I'm not sure. But there are picture-book cafés here and things like that," I reply vaguely.

Saya has been helping out at her family's hardware store ever since she finished high school. She has this idea of me as some kind of sophisticate who can teach her everything about the mysterious world of big city life.

34

"You're amazing, Tomoka. A rising star—going off to Tokyo to become a career woman."

"It's not like that," I protest. Saya's innocent straight-forward chatter is like a mirror reflecting the meanness of my own heart. I told her off the top of my head once that I was in "the fashion business." It's not exactly a lie, and my job does involve clothes. But I didn't mention Eden because, if I had, she would have googled it and discovered the truth.

The reason I can't brush Saya off is not out of friend-ship so much as because she puts me on a pedestal and calls me "amazing" all the time. I probably just want someone to whom I can put on a brave face, and Saya presents me with an image of how I would like to be seen.

When I was at college, her admiration made me feel good. It helped light my fire. But lately I've grown tired of being called "amazing."

I put my chopsticks down and, to atone for my sins, spend the next two hours listening to Saya drone on about her boyfriend.

～

Next morning I oversleep and race out of the door without even brushing my hair or putting on any makeup.

I had ended up fiddling around on my smartphone after I went to bed and then couldn't sleep. I shouldn't have started watching video clips of my favorite idols... Just my luck that today I'm on the early shift.

At work I am tidying a lower shelf while trying to stifle a yawn when I hear an angry voice above my head.

"There you are! I want a word with you!"

The sound is so piercing it nearly bursts my eardrums. Still crouching, I look up to see a woman with tousled hair glaring down at me with her arms folded across her chest. It's the customer from a few days ago who asked if I liked the mulberry or the brown knitted top. Yikes. I stand up in a hurry. She shoves the mulberry top at me.

"What were you doing trying to push a reject like this on me?"

Blood drains from my face. *Reject?*

"When I put it through the washing machine, it shrank! So now I'm returning it and I want my money back!"

For a moment I feel dizzy but now my blood is up and I can't help letting it show in my voice. "Items that have been washed cannot be returned."

"I only bought it because you recommended it! Take responsibility for your own actions!"

My thoughts spin while I try and calm myself. I'd had some experience with customer complaints before, but never a witch like this... I must have learned something during training. What am I supposed to do…? But the anger overrides everything and my mind is a blank—for the life of me, I can't think of an appropriate response.

"You were trying to make a fool out of me by selling an inferior product."

"I was not!"

"I can't talk to you. Get your boss here!"

Something clicks in my brain. If anybody is trying to make a fool out of somebody, it's her. And if we can get my boss involved, I'm all for it. Too bad Mr. Ueshima is not around. He's on the late shift.

"He won't be here until the afternoon."

"Is that so. Well. I'll be back this afternoon."

The customer eyes my name tag. "Fujiki—got it!" she snaps, and storms off.

~

So there I am, the budding career woman and local girl made good, crying and shaking with anger. This is not how I ever want Saya to see me. I didn't bust my gut studying to get away from the sticks and come to Tokyo for this.

When Mr. Ueshima arrives after midday, I report the incident.

"Just tread carefully, would you," he says with a frown.

I wasn't expecting much, but seriously… A renewed anger rises up in me.

Just then Mrs. Numauchi happens to walk by. Sheesh. I don't want *her* to know. I couldn't stand being thought of as incompetent by her as well.

By break time, I am still fuming. I have not eaten since I'd been running late that morning and didn't have time to buy any lunch. I thought I had a packet of sweet snacks in my bag but then remember I'd eaten them two days ago. So now I don't know what to do about lunch. We're not allowed to go into the food section in our uniforms, nor hang around outside. I feel trapped. Like my toes inside my pumps.

I don't feel like getting changed to go outside and I no longer have any appetite. Catching sight of the emergency exit, I wonder if it even opens. I try the handle and the door opens with a creak. Which is good because it is supposed to be an emergency exit. The wind gusts in and I quickly step outside.

"Oh," I say.

"Oh," says Kiriyama at the same time. He is sitting on a landing of the fire escape with his feet on the steps below.

"You caught me," he says with a laugh, removing his earbuds. He must have been listening to music while reading his book. Beside him is a bottle of iced tea and two small round packages wrapped in aluminum foil.

"What's up?" he asks. "Escaping?"

"I could ask you the same thing."

"I'm a regular here. When I want to be alone and stuff. And today is beautiful autumn weather." He points at the packages. "Want a rice ball? If you don't mind homemade."

"You made them?"

"Yeah. I already ate the salmon, so the best is gone. But there's grilled cod roe or konbu, if you want."

All of a sudden I feel hungry.

"Um, grilled cod roe, please."

"Have a seat," Kiriyama says.

Taking the package, I peel off the foil and the rice ball emerges wrapped in another layer of clear plastic wrap.

"So you cook," I remark.

"I do now," Kiriyama says.

I bite into the rice ball. It's delicious. The rice has just the right amount of saltiness, and the small moist beads of grilled cod roe cling together in perfect combination with the rice packed firmly around them. Coral pink wrapped in white. I eat happily without speaking.

"Glad you seem to like it," Kiriyama says with a smile.

All of a sudden I have my mojo back. I didn't know it was possible to recover so quickly.

"This rice ball is amazing."

"Yep sure is, *totally* amazing."

I look at him, surprised by the heatedness of his response.

"Eating is important, you know," he tells me. "Work hard and eat properly."

Wow, is that real emotion I hear in his voice. "Kiriyama, why did you quit your job at the publishing company?"

He begins peeling away the foil from the remaining rice ball. "It wasn't a publishing company, it was an editorial production company. There were only ten of us on the staff."

I've never thought about it before, but other companies put out magazines, not just publishing houses. There are all sorts of companies and jobs out there. I am so ignorant.

"We did all kinds of things," Kiriyama says, "not just magazines. Flyers, pamphlets—stuff like that. Even did a bit of filming. The boss rushed into everything. He took on every single job that came along, without consulting us, the staff—the ones that actually did the work. We were always exhausted. It was taken for granted we'd work all night, and sometimes I put my coat on the floor to sleep or went without a bath for three days in a row."

Kiriyama smiles and a faraway look comes into his eyes.

"I believed that was just how things were in that industry. And I thought I was so hot working on a magazine... But I was wrong."

He pauses while he chews his way through his rice ball. I keep quiet too.

"I had no time to eat and my health was shit. I used to rely on nutrition drinks and supplements. Then one day I was looking at them lying all around my desk when I suddenly thought—what am I working for?" He tosses the last of the rice ball into his mouth. "I was working in order to eat, but I never had time to eat because of work—that seemed crazy."

With one hand, Kiriyama screws up the foil and sighs. "That was good!" he says. "Now I actually have a life. A decent life. I eat properly, sleep, and enjoy reading books and magazines because I don't have to think about them from a work point of view. I'm fit, healthy, and every day is a new beginning."

He sounds very happy.

"I had no idea magazine production was so tough."

"Nah, not every company's like that. I just happened to land in one which operates that way. Besides, I don't want to diss the others doing their best in that company. There are people who can work at that pace and keep themselves in good shape. People who find it fulfilling to completely immerse themselves in work and nothing else. It just wasn't me."

Kiriyama takes a long sip of cold tea.

"But where you are now, at a glasses shop, that's completely different. Weren't you worried whether you'd like it or not?" I ask hesitantly.

"I wrote an article for the magazine once, for a feature on glasses. I did a lot of in-depth research and found it really interesting, so that might be why I accepted the offer for an interview. Then it turned out that the interviewer had read my article and the conversation went really well. He knew the glasses designer I had interviewed." Kiriyama glows at this memory.

"That's not something you can plan. It made me think I ought to focus on what I had in front of me. Then maybe my efforts would pay off in unexpected ways and help me make new connections. To be honest, I didn't start at ZAZ thinking I had my future all mapped out. You can decide things, but there's no guarantee everything will go as planned. It's just that—" Kiriyama's voice breaks off and he pauses. "In a world where you don't know what will happen next, I just do what I can right now."

He sounds like he is talking to himself, not me.

～

When I return from my break, Mr. Ueshima is not around. I ask other staff members and learn that he had announced he was going to do a stock check and hasn't returned. He's run away, I know it. But there is nothing I can do.

After two, the customer comes back. "Where's your boss?" she demands.

I brace myself. Accepting a return is out of the question, but how am I going to convince her? At this precise moment, the thing in front of me that I must deal with is this customer.

I am racking my brains when Mrs. Numauchi, who I thought was supposed to be behind the till, appears at my side.

"Can I be of assistance?"

Mistaking Mrs. Numauchi for my boss, the customer starts firing off her complaints. The way she tells it, there is no doubt that this is all my fault.

Mrs. Numauchi listens with a serious expression, opening her mouth only to say things like "I see," "Yes" and "Is that so?"

When the customer has finished saying her piece, Mrs. Numauchi comments mildly: "Well, knits do shrink if you put them through the washing machine. You must have been quite surprised."

The customer doesn't know what to say. Mrs. Numauchi turns the top inside out and shows her the washing instructions tag. It has a diagram of a hand inside a bucket that means *hand wash*.

"I often make that mistake too, you know. I forget to check the washing instructions and end up putting some delicate item through a machine wash."

"Oh... I, er..."

"But there is a way to fix it, you know," Mrs. Numauchi continues. Then she proceeds to explain in a wonderfully upbeat way what that is exactly. "Just put a small amount of hair conditioner—one pump is enough—in a basin of warm water, dissolve it and immerse the sweater. As soon as it is wet through, take it out again, wring and stretch it into shape, then lay it flat to dry.

"This knitted top is an extremely popular item and this was the last one. The magenta is quite unusual. You don't see many garments in this color."

"Magenta?" The customer's ears prick up. She's looking less scary now.

"Yes, this color."

Suddenly, in her mind, the mulberry top is transformed into a high-fashion item. Magenta...uh-huh. That's certainly one way of putting it.

"This design is a lovely simple one that goes nicely with many pieces. You'll never go wrong with this top. The neckline is plain, and the color is one you can wear right up to the beginning of spring."

"So—I just wash it in hair conditioner and stretch it back into shape?"

"That's right. I believe that would do the trick. Look after it and it will last you a long time."

Mrs. Numauchi is now in complete control of the conversation. Right before my eyes, she has brought the customer around from demanding a return and refund.

Still smiling, she delivers the final punch. "If you have any further concerns, please leave your contact number," she says crisply. "I will ask the staff member in charge to be in touch."

The customer shrinks back: "No, no that won't be necessary."

Nice one! Beat that if you can, lady.

Mrs. Numauchi continues chatting in a friendly way with the customer, who happily starts talking about herself as if all is forgiven. Apparently she'd bought the sweater to wear to a lunch with a friend who she hadn't seen for ten years. It had been such an exhausting journey by train, and she feels awkward in big stores and doesn't have any confidence in her taste anyway. But now she wants to purchase something else as a finishing touch for her outfit.

Mrs. Numauchi signals for me to go back to the till while she hangs on. She recommends a scarf, even including a short lesson on how to tie it, and concludes the sale. I can see even from a distance that the scarf is a perfect match with the mulberry top. The day that customer gets ready to go to her lunch, I bet she will look at herself in the mirror and smile. Then off she'll go in a good mood to meet her old friend.

Way to go, Mrs. Numauchi! I feel so dumb now for telling the librarian that my job in the womenswear section at Eden was "nothing great." *I* haven't been doing a great job, that's all. The day that customer first appeared, I was so itching to take my break I didn't give her my complete attention and I'm sure she sensed it.

When the customer comes over to pay for her scarf at the till, she says, "Thank you," and goes off holding her purchase with a smile on her face. The happy smile of a satisfied customer.

Mrs. Numauchi and I both bow to her. Once she's out of sight, I turn to Mrs. Numauchi and give a deep bow of apology.

"Thank you so much!"

She smiles at me. "Customers in that kind of situation like to feel they've been listened to, and understood. Otherwise they become unhappy."

I feel so ashamed of myself. What had I been thinking until now about Mrs. Numauchi? That I was above her because I was permanent and she was only a part-timer? Deep inside, I know I looked down on her out of a warped sense of superiority at being a permanent employee, and young. I'd been on a stupid ego trip thinking I was better than her, and the woman in the canteen, come to think of it.

I just want to hide. Looking down, I say to Mrs. Numauchi, "I have a lot to learn."

She shakes her head. "At first, I knew nothing, but stick with it and you'll learn along the way. That's all that's needed."

After twelve years she looks completely at ease in her coral-pink blouse. She's amazing, I think, from the bottom of my heart.

≈

That day I am on the early shift, so I leave at four. Once I'm out of uniform it occurs to me that I could go and check out the food section. Catching up with Kiriyama had made me feel like I wanted to cook something too.

I can't think of what to make, though. Pasta, something like that? But I can't decide what type of sauce to make with it and decide to buy an instant one. That's when I put my hand in the pocket of my jacket and find something soft in there. The felt frying pan. It'd been there ever since Ms. Komachi gave it to me. This gives me an idea. I know what I'll make—yellow castella, just like in *Guri and Gura*.

∼

Going into a McDonald's near the food section, I buy a hundred-yen coffee and search online for castella recipes. When I tap in *Gura and Gura castella*, it's incredible how many hits there are. So many people have been inspired by this book to make castella! And the more sites I look at, the more I realize there is no set way of making it—amounts and methods differ from recipe to recipe. Then I come across a very simple one, only a few lines long. It involves no sifting of flour or separating of eggs. "I made this faithfully following how it was made in the book," say the instructions. It looks like something even I could do. Something I could do right now.

The website recipe requires a frying pan, mixing bowl and whisk, along with three eggs, 60g flour, 60g sugar, 20g butter, melted, and 30ml milk. An 18cm-diameter frying pan seems best, with a lid. And though the recipe doesn't say so, I need scales and a measuring cup. I'm embarrassed to think I have almost none of these in my apartment. But the brilliant thing is—I can get them all at Eden!

∼

I haven't cooked in the kitchen in a lo-o-ong time. First I break the eggs into the bowl, add the sugar and mix them together with the whisk. Then I add the melted butter and the milk... Already the mixture smells so sweet and delicious. I can't believe it—I am actually baking a cake!

Next, the flour. I mix that in, beating the whisk super efficiently around and around in the bowl. Then I place the frying pan on the gas ring, melt some more butter and pour in the batter. I put the lid on and turn the flame down very low to steam the mixture. Now all I have to do is wait thirty minutes, while checking every now and then. My stove has only one ring, but luckily it's gas. I feel sure it will go well. Fancy being able to make castella in this tiny kitchen!

You are so amazing, Tomoka, I tell myself. I raise my clenched fists in a victory pose. Oops—my hands are still covered in flour. As I wash them in the basin, I glance at myself in the mirror, then take a good look at what I see. My skin is awful. Probably because all I ever eat is cup ramen and savory rolls from convenience stores, and my fridge has no real food in it, only a jumble of condiments all past their use-by date. And I'm pale from lack of sleep, too. No wonder I don't have much energy.

As I look around my tiny apartment, it's clear that diet isn't my only problem. Dust coats the floor and the windows are so dirty I can barely see through them. There are clothes hanging everywhere because I've fallen into the habit of leaving washed clothes out to take straight from the hangers to wear instead of putting them away. My shelves are a mess of assorted objects: bottles of nail polish gone hard; three-month-old TV magazines; a yoga DVD I'd bought six months ago on a whim and never even opened.

It dawns on me that I have not been looking after myself. I don't care about what I put in my mouth, or my surroundings, and I treat myself carelessly. Like Kiriyama, but for different reasons, I too have not been living a decent life.

After washing my hands thoroughly, I give the apartment a quick clean while waiting for the castella to cook. I fold up laundry and run the vacuum cleaner over the floor. Once I start, my body seems to move by itself. In my mind it always seems like a huge task to do cleaning, but when I actually get down to it, the small one-room apartment scrubs up well in no time. Easy-peasy!

Mmmm…the sweet smell of baking fills my beautifully clean space. I check the castella and see the batter beginning to rise so well it looks like it might lift the lid off.

"Amazing!" I whoop at the sight of it, looking so fluffy and golden. Just like the picture in the book!

I can't resist lifting up the lid for a peek. The edges are already setting, but there are air bubbles in the center, which still looks runny, so I set the lid down again.

Maybe I am a teeny bit closer to leading a decent life now. I sit on the floor, leaning against the wall, and open up *Guri and Gura*—two field mice who go deep into the forest.

"When our basket is full of acorns, let's boil them with lots of sugar," says Guri.

"When our basket is full of chestnuts, let's boil them till they're soft enough to make chestnut cream," says Gura.

Oh, I sigh. Guri and Gura didn't go into the forest to look for an egg, let alone make castella. They went looking for acorns and chestnuts, food that they ate every day. Just like they always did. And unexpectedly, they found a giant egg. I remember Saya saying, "If you don't know what to do with an egg in the first place, you wouldn't think of castella." She's right. Now I get it. When they found the egg, they knew what it could be used for, because they already knew how to make castella.

Yes! My heart sings as I realize I may have hit on some truth. In high hopes I head back to the stove. Mmm, the smell of baking is even stronger now.

I open the lid, and gasp. The edges of the batter are black where it has overcooked in the pan, and where I was expecting to see a fluffy center is a sunken cavity. In shock I turn it on to a plate with a spatula. The bottom is burned, and the moment I remove it from the frying pan, it sinks even more in the middle. The gluggy mass spreads stickily out sideways.

"Eww…?"

I break off a piece to try. It doesn't taste at all like castella. This is glutinous and tough, like rubber. What did I do wrong? I can't understand it. I thought I followed the recipe exactly.

While chewing on an overly sweet horrible lump, it suddenly strikes me as funny and I fall about laughing. I'm not devastated; if anything I feel good. What's to cry about when I have a tidy apartment and a sink full of cooking utensils.

I will not give up. I can learn how to do this thing.

~

From then on, every day for a week after coming home from work, I make castella cake. It becomes part of my daily routine, almost an obsession.

I search online for tips to improve it. Letting the eggs reach room temperature first. Placing the frying pan on a damp cloth from time to time during cooking to take the edge off the heat. These really help. But I am still nowhere near achieving the soft fluffy texture of my dreams.

By this stage, all the steps that I couldn't be bothered with in the beginning—sifting the flour and separating the eggs to make meringue with the egg whites and sugar—didn't seem like such a hassle anymore. So I buy another utensil for my kitchen: a flour sifter. Getting the hang of making meringue isn't an easy process but so worth it as the batter becomes much smoother. Still not smooth enough, though. I am determined to do better. I end up buying a hand mixer as well, because I just have to make a good meringue.

Another important factor is the cooking temperature. I had it fixed in my brain that the flame should be kept low, so it takes me a while to realize I need to adjust it and to work out when to cool the pan. You have to do stuff like that for yourself to really get the hang of it.

But keep at it and you'll learn along the way. *This* is what Mrs. Numauchi had been trying to tell me!

Something else changes. I spend so much time in the kitchen, I begin to cook dinner as well. Just simple stuff. Compared to making castella, it's a cinch to cut up vegetables and meat to simmer or stir-fry. The rice cooker takes care of making rice. I put any leftovers in a Tupperware container to make rice balls for work. Kiriyama got a huge surprise when he saw me eating one during my break. I was pretty surprised myself. It is amazing how much more energy I have and how much healthier I feel after only a few days.

Today, the big moment finally arrives, the seventh day, when I lift the lid on the frying pan and receive the reward for all my persistence. *Yes!* I nod in satisfaction.

"The yellow castella showed its soft spongy face," I announce out loud.

I break off a piece while it is still in the frying pan and, just like in the book, pop it into my mouth. Yum! It's delicious—so light and fluffy. *I did it!* I baked a castella that would make all the creatures in the forest open their eyes. Tears well in my own. I promise myself that, from now on, I really will try to eat properly.

~

"Wow, this is amazing!" Kiriyama exclaims loudly when I give him some of my castella. Like he really means it. I decide to believe him.

I'd wanted to thank him for the rice ball he gave me before, and I'd wanted to see him smile. When it dawns on me that might be the reason I tried so hard, my heart skips a beat.

There is one more person I have to thank—Mrs. Numauchi. After work the same day, I give her some castella in the locker room and tell her how much I appreciated her help.

"I copied Guri and Gura to make this," I say.

She bursts out laughing. "*Guri and Gura*! I loved that story when I was a girl. I read it so many times."

"Really? When you were young?" I say, my eyes wide in surprise.

"Hey, I was young once too, you know," she says, pouting in make-believe offense.

I suppose so. But I can't imagine it.

It's amazing the power stories can have. Old favorites such as *Guri and Gura*, which never change, though generation after generation have grown up reading them.

Mrs. Numauchi seems miles away, as if she is thinking about something. "I... The thing I liked about that book is that they have to deal with all these tricky problems."

Puzzled, I tilt my head. "Is that what it's about?"

She gives a big nod. "Of course. They can't carry the egg because it's too big and smooth, then the shell is hard to crack. The frying pan won't fit in their backpacks—they have to deal with one thing after another, don't they?"

When I'd told Kiriyama about *Gura and Gura*, he'd said, "That's the story about animals in the forest getting together to eat cake, isn't it?" For such a short book, it's interesting how everybody remembers it differently.

In the locker room, Mrs. Numauchi keeps talking. "The two mice think about their options—should we do this or should we do that—and in the end they decide to cooperate. That's the part I like most." She gives me a big smile.

~

Next day is Wednesday, my day off, so I go back to the library in the Community House. The two-week loan period for my books is up and I need to return them. I have my felted frying pan from Ms. Komachi attached to a strap hanging from my bag. It's become my good-luck charm.

I return the books to Nozomi and then I go to see Ms. Komachi. She's in the same place, squished between the L-shaped counter and partition, still doing the thing with her felting needle. Poking in and out, in and out, the ball of wool under her hands gradually taking shape and turning into another felt mascot.

When I stand in front of her, she stops and looks up at me. I bow. "Thank you. For *Guri and Gura*, and for the frying pan… I learned something important."

"Oh?" Ms. Komachi looks at me, her head on one side. "I did nothing. You took what you needed, yourself," she says in that laid-back way of hers.

I point to the orange box. "Honeydome cookies are really delicious, aren't they?"

Suddenly she blushes and looks happy. "They *are* good. I love them. They make everybody happy."

I give a big nod to that.

~

It's time for computer class, so I head for the meeting room. I think that I might be just entering the forest. I still don't know what I want to do, or what I can do. What I do know is that there's no need to panic, or do more than I can cope with right now. For the time being, I plan to simply get my life in order and learn some new skills, choosing from what's available. I'll prepare myself, like Guri and Gura gathering chestnuts in the forest.

Because I never know when I might find my own giant egg.

2

Ryo, 35, accounts department of
a furniture manufacturer

It all began with a spoon. A small, flat-handled, silver spoon that caught my eye on a shelf. I picked it up for a closer look and saw a tulip-like chevron on the end with an engraved sheep design. It was a teaspoon, I guessed, from the size.

I lingered a while to gaze at it, then continued browsing through the dimly lit shop, still holding it in my hand. The shelves were crowded with old bric-a-brac: pocket watches, candlesticks, glass bottles, insect specimens and indeterminate bones; screws, nails and locks. Numerous dingy objects, caught in time's deep embrace, waited expectantly under the light of a naked bulb.

I was a high-school student at the time. That day I had got off the train one stop early and was taking a detour to avoid going straight home because of a minor spat with my mother in the morning. As I wandered the streets of the city on the edges of Kanagawa Prefecture, I came across a shop set slightly apart from the main business district, with a sandwich-board sign propped outside the entrance. "ENMOKUYA," it read. *Smoke Tree*. From what I could make out through the window, it looked like an antique shop. On a whim, I went inside.

A long-faced, middle-aged man in a knitted cap, whom I took to be the owner, was behind the till. He had the same fusty air as his stock, which is often the case with proprietors of shops that sell old things. While I was looking around, he fiddled about with a clock and then a music box, not appearing to pay any attention to me.

The spoon in my hand became warm from my body heat and melded snugly against my palm. After some hesitation, I bought it for 1,500 yen. That was a lot of money for a high-school student to pay for one spoon. I had no idea of its value, but I couldn't bring myself to put it back on the shelf.

"This is pure silver," the man in the cap told me. "It's a teaspoon, made in England."

"When was it made?" I asked.

He put on reading glasses to scrutinize the back of the spoon: "In 1905."

When I looked for myself, all I could see were four

marks consisting of letters and pictures, none of which were numerals.

"How can you tell?"

The owner of the shop chuckled and smiled for the first time—a genuine smile that made me warm to him even though he hadn't answered my question. He was plainly passionate about antiques and confident of his own eye. Both the shop and its owner left quite an impression on me. I thought they were pretty cool.

I took the spoon home and tried to imagine its history. Who had owned it in England in the 1900s? What did people eat with it? Maybe an aristocratic lady had placed it daintily on her saucer during afternoon tea. Or maybe a mother fed her young son with it, bringing the spoon gently up to his mouth, and long after he had grown stout and middle-aged, he still remembered that spoon with affection. Or maybe it had been in a family of three girls who fought over it at every meal. Maybe…

My imagination ran wild. I never grew bored of looking at my spoon.

After that I often dropped by Enmokuya on my way home after school. The owner's name was Mr. Ebigawa, I learned. He wore a knitted cap all year round: wool in winter and autumn, and cotton or hemp in summer and spring.

Enmokuya was a place where I could forget everything. All the petty worries of daily life, troubles at school, Mom's nagging, anxieties about my future—no matter how stressed out I felt, all I had to do was open that door to step into another world. It was a place where I could be myself; where I was accepted for who I was. Usually, all I did was look, which I felt bad about, but I did buy a few small things with the limited resources of my pocket money.

In time, Mr. Ebigawa and the regular customers opened up and started talking to me. They taught me the history and language of antiques. After I'd been frequenting his shop for about a year, Mr. Ebigawa taught me about hallmarks, which is what the four marks on the back of my spoon were called. They indicated the maker's mark, the purity mark, the assay office mark and the date of manufacture.

"This box with the letter 'n' tells us it was made in 1905."

I learned to identify the combination of letters and boxes used in place of numbers. That was such an English sensibility, I thought, to use a system like this instead of ordinary numbers.

My spoon felt even more precious after Mr. Ebigawa told me that the sheep was probably a family crest, or perhaps just one part of it. The sheep wasn't just decorative—it was a sign of respect for the family's lineage! That seemed so cool. I was infatuated with the antique world and in awe of Mr. Ebigawa.

~

Today, Enmokuya no longer exists. One day, not long before I finished high school, I arrived to find a handwritten notice posted on the door that read "Store Closed" and with that my relationship with Mr. Ebigawa came to an abrupt end.

I never went through its door again. That was eighteen years ago. Maybe that's why I've always yearned to have my own shop, just like Enmokuya. *One day.* Even now at the age of thirty-five, I still dream of it.

One day when I have enough money saved up, I will quit my job, find somewhere to open a shop and curate the shelves... *One day...*

But will *one day* ever come?

~

After university I left home and started working in the accounts department of a furniture manufacturer. It's not a big company, nor does it make expensive products, but the constant demand for reasonably priced informal furniture means that business is stable.

"How do you do this again?" my boss, Mr. Taguchi, the department chief, twists around in his seat to ask.

Not again, I think. He asked the same thing yesterday. The company recently introduced a whole raft of new software that is beyond Mr. Taguchi's grasp. Every time he gets stuck, he asks me. Despite being in the middle of an expenditures check, I stop what I am doing. Standing behind his chair, I explain what to do.

"Aha, aha, so that's how it's done!" he says loudly, exaggeratedly moving his rubbery lips. "Thanks for helping, Urase. You really know your stuff."

I return to my desk and resume the expenditures check. I like working with numbers. Our job in the accounts department is to keep track of the company's finances rather than manage them, so the work is not that difficult, and there's no risk. It's dry, unexciting work that doesn't require great passion. Easy enough, if you like that kind of thing.

"Urase, how about a drink tomorrow? We could go to the same place as last month. They're discounting beer for their third anniversary," Mr. Taguchi calls out.

I glance at the bundle of receipts in my hand. "Sorry, but I'm taking a day off tomorrow."

"Oh, right."

Luckily I had an excuse ready. Mr. Taguchi likes to talk, so going out with him can be tedious. Not that I'm brave enough to pass over every invitation from my boss. But with end-of-year parties coming up, when I'll have to show my face, I have good reason to avoid any invitations now as much as possible.

Mr Taguchi spins around on his chair to face me and leans in close. "Date with your girlfriend?"

"I guess you could say that."

"Hah, I thought so. My bad luck." He slaps himself on the forehead theatrically.

I laugh dutifully while inwardly cursing myself for giving away too much.

Mr. Taguchi looks at me pointedly and smirks. "You've been seeing this girl quite a while. Getting hitched soon?"

"Oh, what's this?" I say, changing the subject. "These figures don't add up. Looks like Amano in the sales department again. He always messes up; I'll have to get him to redo them." I look at Mr. Taguchi with a forced smile. "I really don't understand why people can't do their expenses reports properly."

Mr. Taguchi laughs and turns back to his screen.

The internal phone line rings. Miss Yoshitaka, my twenty-something assistant who has only recently started at the company, reaches over with a weary air from her desk opposite mine to pick up. After a few brusque words, she presses hold and turns to me: "Mr. Urase, call for you."

"Oh, who from?"

"A man. Didn't get his name."

I look at her with surprise. "Thanks," I say, and pick up the receiver.

The call is from the overseas operations department. The company is preparing to import some new interior furnishings from the UK, and we in Accounts have been asked to prepare a draft budget. Mr. Taguchi is in charge of handling this, but for some reason I am always the one people in other departments ask for. Probably so they can enjoy pushing me around.

I press hold and turn to Mr. Taguchi. "Is the draft budget for the UK brand ready? Apparently it's needed for a meeting tomorrow."

"Ah, that—I couldn't finish it. All those pounds instead of dollars. Couldn't get my head around it. And I'm not as good at English as you are, Urase," he says, fixing me with a faux pleading look.

My heart drops. "Don't worry, I'll do it," I reply after a beat.

"Appreciate it. I owe you." Mr. Taguchi raises one hand in acknowledgment.

Meanwhile, Miss Yoshitaka is trimming her split ends.

That about sums up my workplace: I have an incompetent boss and an assistant with attitude. It could be worse, I know, but it's at times like this that I want to quit.

I have a hard time knowing how to deal with people. It's a good thing I was assigned to Accounts, my first choice, and not somewhere like Sales. But I know that no matter where I work, the stress of human relations is not something I can easily escape.

My dream is to quit this job and open my own shop. I'd fill it with the things I like, and never have to talk with anybody except customers who are like-minded antique lovers. But I can't quit. I have less than one million yen saved up, which is not enough to start a business, and with all the work I have to do, it's impossible to find the time for the necessary study and prep. But time is slipping away while I'm stuck in this office grind.

Will it ever be possible to walk through the door of my very own antique shop? The only thing I am sure of is that tonight I will have to do overtime again.

∽

The next day, Wednesday, I go to pick up Hina. Hina is my girlfriend, and she lives at home with her parents in a quiet residential area. As I approach the house, she sticks her head out of the window of her bedroom upstairs and affectionately calls out, "Ryo!" She must have been watching out for me. I stand waiting in the garden, expecting her to come down immediately. Instead, however, Hina's mother appears on the doorstep.

"Ryo, we haven't seen you for a while. You're looking well."

"Oh, hello."

"You'll stay for dinner today?"

"Er...okay. You're always too kind."

"It's no trouble. My husband enjoys your company. Would you prefer fish or meat? Hina doesn't eat fish, so I always like to cook it whenever I have..."

Hina bounces out of the door. "Mom, enough. You've already said too much."

Linking her arm through mine, she waves to her mother with her free hand and pulls me after her. Her scent smells like vanilla.

There's a ten-year age gap between Hina and me. She's only twenty-five. We met three years ago when I was walking on Yuigahama beach at Kamakura after I'd been to a flea market at one of the temples. She was crouched down on the sand, sifting through it with such a serious expression that I thought she must have lost something important. When I asked if everything was all right, she replied that she was collecting sea glass. She told me that she used it to make accessories, and in the Tupperware container next to her she already had an assortment of green and blue glass, along with shells and dried starfish.

Sea glass is the glass from faraway places that you find washed up on the beach. Fragments of broken jars and bottles are tossed by the waves until the edges rub smooth, and they arrive on the shores of other countries looking like nature's own polished works of art.

"It's so romantic to think this glass was part of something once used by somebody far away, a long time ago. I get so caught up trying to imagine who might've used it and where and when, I can't stop thinking about it."

Like me, I thought. She sees the world the same way I do, with the same eye. I squatted down beside her to look in the sand and spotted all kinds of things: desiccated seaweed, pieces of driftwood, pebbles, a single beach sandal, plastic bags, bottle caps. The kind of flotsam that mostly gets labeled as garbage. Yet from another perspective, these are treasures, and the beach is one vast foraging ground for finding such things.

I spotted a small fragment of glass that was red and shaped like a broad bean. "What about this?" I asked, handing it to her.

Hina made a strangled sound in her throat and her

eyes widened in surprise. "It's beautiful! Red is quite rare. This is wonderful—thank you so much."

I nodded, as if to say, "You're welcome," then hurriedly said goodbye. She was charming, but I felt so self-conscious I didn't know what to say. I suppose sometimes I do get lucky. But I didn't think anything more of it at the time.

However, that was not the end of it. Next weekend we met again completely by accident. This time it was at an antique market in the Tokyo Big Sight exhibition center, where by some miracle I ran into her among the hundreds of booths and thronging crowds. It's sort of embarrassing to say this, but it was like the air around her glowed. When I saw her, I couldn't help calling out. It was on the spur of the moment—I didn't even stop to think. Hina was astonished too. We chatted for a bit and then I asked her to have tea with me. Until then, I had not once ever made a pass at a girl. I've gone over that moment in my head many times since, and it still amazes me that I did such a thing.

We share a passion for old things. It makes us kindred spirits, and we spend our time seeking out shops to visit and events to attend together. Occasionally, we talk about having our own shop one day. But it is just daydreaming, and *one day* means after I retire, or we win the lottery. I'm sure Hina has no idea how serious I am about wanting to make that dream come true. Retirement is still many years off for me, and I worry that by the time it comes around, I won't have the passion, strength or funds to run a business anymore.

Today we're going to hear a lecture entitled "Fun with Minerals" at a community center that Hina discovered in her neighborhood. Apparently it's next to an elementary school, but not the one she attended. "So I did well to find it," she told me. "I came across it when I was looking for a computer course to help me run an online shop. It's great value—only 2,000 yen for two hours of virtually individual instruction. I go regularly now. The Community House is an amazing place, with so many different lectures, classes and activities."

No longer content with simply making sea-glass accessories, Hina is now thinking of how to sell them too. She doesn't have to worry about making a living to support herself as she has a part-time job in an office three days a week and lives at home. She has plenty of time to spare for making accessories and running an online shop. Not like me.

I shake my head and chastise myself. Don't be mean.

We arrive at the Community House, which turns out to be a white building that's separate from the school. We enter and record our names, purpose of visit and time of arrival on a sheet of paper at the reception desk.

I note that ten people have been in before us that morning to use a meeting room, the Japanese-style room and the library. The fact this place has a library surprises me.

The lecture is in Meeting Room B with an audience of four. Besides us, there are two older men. But maybe a small audience is just right for this type of talk.

The speaker is a man in his fifties called Mr. Mogi, who begins by introducing himself. He tells us that he works at a mineral processing plant, where he became so interested in minerals that it has become his hobby as well. He qualified as a mineral appraiser and gives talks and conducts field trips almost wholly on a voluntary basis whenever he has time.

Humph. His hobby is an all-consuming passion and he does these things voluntarily. Good for him. I'm sure he doesn't bother anyone doing that.

These ungenerous thoughts are not distracting enough for me to find the talk uninteresting. Mr. Mogi talks about the different kinds of minerals and how they are formed; he shows us specimens of rare minerals and how to use a loupe correctly. Then he hands us each a stone about five centimeters long with graduated purple and yellow stripes. "This is fluorite, from Argentina," he tells us. "We're going to polish it."

We drip water on our stones with a pipette and polish them with sandpaper. Once they are smooth, we rinse them in water and then give them a final polish with a finer grade of sandpaper. Once the unevenness is smoothed away, the stripes stand out vividly.

I can picture doing this in my dream shop. I could have a corner devoted to minerals, and invite experts to come and give talks at small, intimate events…

When the ninety minutes are up, Hina asks if I mind waiting while she speaks with the teacher. "I'd like to try making accessories with minerals too, so I want to ask about the hardness and suitability of particular stones."

Hina certainly is ambitious for her online shop. There is no reason for me to stand in her way. "Sure, there's a library here, so I'll go and look at books or something. Take your time."

～

The library at the end of the passageway is larger than I expected, with rows and rows of bookshelves lining the walls and central area. Apart from a girl in a navy-blue apron behind the counter, who is scanning barcodes on books, there is nobody else in there as far as I can tell.

I browse through the shelves along the wall closest to the door. As the Community House is located so close to an elementary school, I assumed its collection would be weighted toward a juvenile readership, but am surprised to discover that the range of books is equal to that of any standard library.

I look for books about antiques and quickly find them in the arts and crafts section. After flipping through a few, I decide to look for books on how to open a shop. The girl in the apron walks past with several books in her hands. Reshelving them, I expect.

"Excuse me, do you have anything about business start-ups and management?" I ask her.

She looks startled. "Er, um... That would be in business, maybe. But biographies of business people might be useful too."

The name on her badge is Nozomi Morinaga. She looks like a teenager still, and is trying so hard to think, I feel bad. "Oh, don't worry about it," I reassure her, dismissing my request with a wave of my hand.

Nozomi's face turns bright red. "I'm sorry. I'm still a trainee. But there's a librarian in the reference section at the back who you can consult."

In the direction she points I see there is a sign with the word "Reference" on it, hanging from the ceiling. This library might be small, but having a professional librarian is a sign that it is no tinpot facility.

When I make my way to the back and peer over the partition at the reference desk on the other side, I do a double take. Sitting behind the desk is a large woman.

By large, I mean very large. Her head rests on top of a body that looks like it is on the verge of bursting, with no neck visible in between. She wears a beige apron and a loose-knit ivory cardigan, and her skin is ghostly pale. She reminds me of the Stay-Puft Marshmallow Man in *Ghostbusters*.

I approach with care. The expression on Stay-Puft's face is dour—I can see her body is quivering faintly. Is she not well? When I glance down at her hands, I notice them moving busily behind the counter, stabbing with a needle at some kind of round object. What on earth is she doing? Some kind of stress-relief exercise, perhaps?

Still in two minds as to whether to speak to her or not, I am about to turn on my heels when she lifts her head. Our eyes meet unexpectedly, and I freeze.

"What are you looking for?"

Her voice is uncanny. Gentle, with an underlying note of tenderness that is most unexpected in that un-smiling face. My feet move unsteadily toward her, as if of their own accord.

What are you looking for? she had asked me.

I think about it. *A place for these dreams that I don't know what to do with?*

The name badge on Stay-Puft's chest says "Sayuri Komachi." All right, I shall call her Ms. Komachi. I observe a floral ornamental hairpin speared through the bun on her head.

"Er...do you have any books about starting a business?"

"Starting a business," she repeats.

Hearing her repeat my words makes them sound grand, as if I am thinking about embarking on some really impressive project. Sheepishly, I follow up with another request. "And also something with tips on how to successfully resign from a job." Not that I'll ever be able to start a business or quit my job.

Ms. Komachi places the needle and round object in an orange cardboard box, which I recognize as a Kuremiyado Honeydome cookie box. I used to be given these as a reward for helping at home when I was a kid.

She puts the lid on and looks at me. "There are many types of businesses. What is it you want to do?"

"I want to own my own antique shop one day."

"One day."

Once again, she repeats a single phrase of mine in a flat tone.

"Well, of course I can't quit my job anytime soon," I say quickly, feeling the need to justify myself. "And securing the funding to open a shop won't be easy. But the more I say 'one day' the more I feel like it might only ever be a dream."

"Only ever a dream…" She tilts her head to one side inquiringly. "Is that what you think? That it will only ever be a dream? As long as you continue to say the words 'one day,' the dream is not over. Maybe it will simply remain a beautiful dream. It may never come true. But that is one way to live, in my opinion. The days go by more happily when you have something to dream about. It's not always a bad thing to have a dream, with no plan for ever carrying it out."

I am lost for words. If 'one day' are magic words that keep a dream alive, what do I need to say to make it real?

"But if you need to know what lies beyond the dream, you need to know."

Without warning Ms. Komachi sits ramrod straight in her seat and turns to face the computer screen. For a split second she holds her fingers above the keyboard, and then, without preamble, launches into a high-speed blitz on it. Her fingers move so fast they are a blur. I can only gape in astonishment. Finally, with a single flamboyant flourish she hits the return key and a piece of paper begins to emerge from the printer.

I scan the sheet she hands to me. It is a table of book titles with the author names and shelf numbers: *You Too Can Open a Store*, *My Store*, *Seven Things You Should Do Before Quitting Your Job*. The last one on the list, however, is one I have to read twice: *Royal Horticultural Society:*

How Do Worms Work? A Gardener's Collection of Curious Questions and Astonishing Answers.

Surely, this is a mistake. I read the full title aloud. Softly, but loud enough for her to hear. Ms. Komachi, however, gives no reaction and continues to regard me.

"How Do Worms Work?" I repeat.

"Uh-huh." She pats her hairpin. "Incidentally, this flower is acacia."

How am supposed to respond to this? "It's lovely," I reply.

She taps on the lid of the Honeydome box with an index finger. I glance at the picture of a white flower on it and the penny drops. The flower on the Honeydome box is acacia. How is it that I've seen this box numerous times before but never thought about what type of flower that is?

"The honey in Honeydome cookies comes from acacia flowers," she murmurs. Then she folds her large body over to reach down and open the second drawer under the counter.

"And for you—this one. Please, take it." She holds out a hand like a lightly squashed cream bun. I automatically stretch mine out in return and feel something soft and light on my palm. It is a woolen ball that looks like…a cat? A cat with a brown body and black stripes, sleeping on its side. A brown mackerel tabby.

"Um, what's this for?"

78

"It's a free gift."

"Excuse me?"

"A free gift, a bonus to go with the books."

A bonus? And what had she been implying when she said, "And for you"? Do I look like a cat lover? Why?

"These are really so easy to make. You don't need a pattern. And you don't have to make an exact copy of anything," she tells me and, with this, opens the lid of the Honeydome box, takes out the needle and ball of wool, and once more begins to plunge the needle in and out. This feels to me like a signal that my time is up. No more questions. I turn to leave, with the sheet of paper and cat in hand.

"Oh, and one more thing," she says, not looking up. "When you go, don't forget to record the time of your departure in the visitors' log on the front counter. So many people forget to do that."

"Ah, yes, of course."

Prick, prick, prick goes the needle as she jabs it with regular precision, in and out, in and out, her Stay-Puft body quivering with fine vibrations in time with each jab.

～

List in hand, I wander among the bookshelves checking numbers, and have just located all the recommended titles, including the last, when Hina arrives. I was not expecting her to finish so quickly. But perhaps I spent more time talking with Ms. Komachi than I thought.

Her sharp eyes immediately spot the cat mascot and she takes it from me to examine. "What's this?"

"Something the librarian gave me."

"Cute. It's felting."

Felting. So that's what she was doing. I make a gesture to present Hina with the cat, but she pushes it back at me and says, "Are you borrowing books?"

Caught off guard, I take the cat back. "Oh—no, I was just looking," I assure her, swiftly sliding the worm book over the other titles in such a way as to hide them.

"Will you be applying for a borrower's card?" calls out Nozomi, the zealous trainee librarian.

I am about to reply in the negative when Hina jumps in. "Can anybody borrow books?"

"Anyone living in the ward can get a borrower's card."

"Great. He doesn't, but I do."

Hina goes over to the counter. I use the time to hurriedly return the business books to the shelves, and then saunter over with the worm book, as if I have an interest in gardening. *As if.* I hand it to Hina to borrow for me.

We leave the library and head for the front entrance. On the way I recall Ms. Komachi's admonition to record my departure time in the visitors' log. I write it on the sheet of paper and put the pen down. As I do, a pile of leaflets lying on the counter registers in my brain for the first time. The color photocopied A4 sheets scream *handmade* in a way that marks them as intended for Community House patrons. *Hatori CH Newsletter* is the name of the publication. *CH* presumably being an abbreviation for "Community House."

I look at the covering page and blink at what I see. At the bottom of the sheet is a photograph of a cat that looks exactly like the felted one Ms. Komachi has just given me. A man with glasses wearing a horizontal-striped shirt holds the brown tabby in his arms, against a background of rows of bookshelves.

On impulse I pick up a copy of Vol. 31 of the *Hatori CH Newsletter*. Over half of this edition appears to be devoted to a feature on staff recommendations for businesses and shops in the city; it has information on cake shops, flower shops, cafés, pork cutlet restaurants and karaoke clubs. The caption for the photo of the man with the cat reads, "Librarian Sayuri Komachi's top-pick bookshop," and the name of the store is Cats Now Books. Apparently it sells books about cats, and also has real cats actually in the store.

"It looks like rain. Come on, Ryo, let's hurry," Hina calls from the front entrance where she is peering outside.

I fold the newsletter in half and tuck it between the pages of my book, thrust it my bag and follow after her.

~

Hina is the youngest of three girls. The oldest sister, Kimiko, is thirty-five, the same age as me, and the next oldest, Erika, is thirty-two. Hina was apparently an un-expected late addition. Kimiko is single and works as a sound mixer at an Osaka TV station, while Erika is married to a Czech man and lives in Prague. I can well understand why Hina's parents like to cosset their only daughter still living at home.

They have always been fine with Hina staying at my place at the weekend. She is an adult, after all, and they prefer to be open rather than have us lie and pretend. I guess they became a lot more relaxed as parents by their third child.

Ever since I dropped Hina off after a day out driving in a rental car last summer, and was dragged inside their house for dinner, I have gradually been drawn into the family. Hina and I have never spoken about marriage but it is clear her parents are thinking along those lines.

"Busy at work, Ryo?" her father asked on that first occasion, holding out a bottle of beer to refill my glass.

I quickly downed my drink. "Yes, you could say so.

82

Staffing is unpredictable at the moment because of the end-of-year hours adjustment for tax purposes. But I really should be more organized."

"Are you getting lumped with other people's work, Ryo? A nice, hardworking fellow like you—it wouldn't surprise me to hear it," he said, and filled my glass with more beer, which I accepted with a nod.

"Dad, stop forcing beer on Ryo. You know he can't drink a lot," Hina chided him.

In answer, her father laughed and suggested I stay over. "Hina, would you give me a hand, please?" her mother called from the kitchen.

When Hina had left the table, her father reached for a piece of simmered flounder with his chopsticks and said in a low voice, eyes down, "The older girls were always so headstrong, they went off and did exactly as they liked."

He spoke quietly so they couldn't hear us in the kitchen.

"But Hina lives in a world of her own," he went on. "She's always talking like she's in a dream, not quite in the real world. We might have spoiled her too much. But with a steady chap like you at her side, we needn't worry about her."

He was silent a moment, then smiled shyly and looked me in the face. "Please, take care of her."

Unfortunately, I am not the kind of steady fellow who can respond to such a declaration in the affirmative. Instead, I smiled ambiguously, pretending to be shy and embarrassed.

I am grateful they like me, and think of me as a worthy candidate for their precious daughter's hand. Somebody they can trust to protect her for the rest of her life. But that is a heck of a lot of pressure! How could I mention that I'd like to quit my stable job at the company to open an antique shop?

≈

After our excursion to the Community House, I have a shower and lie down with my library book and smartphone.

How Do Worms Work? I pick it up to examine more carefully. The cover has a delicate sketch of worms sandwiched between the title and the subtitle, with its promise of astonishing answers to a gardener's questions. It's a strange and unusual book, yet somehow…enticing.

For the life of me, I cannot think why the librarian would recommend it to me, but evidently she is right because I feel drawn to it. I flip through the pages. The text is presented in a question-and-answer format: easy to read and simple enough for a schoolchild to follow, but in language that is not in the least childish. There are also meticulously drawn botanical illustrations liberally sprinkled throughout.

As I lie on my back with the book open, the Community House newsletter flutters out from between its pages. I pick it up and once again see the photo of the cat bookshop. According to the article, it stocks only cat-related books and donates a portion of its sales to cat-rescue organizations. Rescue cats are also members of staff.

Come to think of it, the two notches of the trefid pattern on my silver spoon make it look a bit like a cat's paw.

I do an online search for Cats Now Books and discover it is located in the Sangenjaya district of Tokyo. Interestingly, there are also hits for several interviews with Yasuhara, the owner, and the shop's Twitter account. The first article I open has a photo of Yasuhara wearing a T-shirt with an image of a cat on it. He is standing in front of the bookshelves holding a cat—a black cat, not the brown tabby. How many cats does this shop have, I wonder?

From a photo of a beer bottle labeled "Wednesday's Cat," I learn that the store also serves beverages. "Cats, books and beer: surrounded by his favorite things," reads the caption. I study the photo of Yasuhara, smiling at the camera.

Lucky guy. Living his dream. I wish I…

My eyes feel heavy. Drowsily, I continue scanning the article. Apparently Yasuhara works for an IT company as well as running this shop. Can you do that? "Social business," "crowdfunding…" Skipping over the unfamiliar jargon, I continue to read. One of Yasuhara's comments puzzles me: "A parallel career means having two careers that are complementary, with neither being secondary to the other."

Neither one is secondary to the other? What does that mean?

As I search for the phrase "parallel career," I come across quotes from a management expert called Peter F. Drucker that are in essence about being active in more than one field. Switching off my smartphone, I stifle a yawn and succumb to sleep.

～

The next day, Miss Yoshitaka is about to leave at five on the dot when I stop her. "Did you finish checking the sales department's expenses report? I've been waiting for it."

"Ah, that. I…er, not yet. I've just painted my nails. Okay if I do it tomorrow?" she says, waving her fingers in the air, apparently under the impression that recently manicured nails are a valid reason for neglecting work.

"The deadline is today," I say, attempting to be reasonable.

She makes a face, as if I have said something outrageous, and flounces back to her desk. Delicately taking her smartphone from her bag—so as not to ruin those nails?—she makes a phone call.

"Hi, sorry but I'll be late. An urgent job just came in."

No doubt she is phoning instead of sending a text or message so that I will hear it. I almost feel sorry for having started this…but, no—why should I feel in the wrong?

I get on with some nonurgent work of my own. She's not the only one with plans. I, too, have somewhere else I want to be right now. But I cannot leave without that expenses report. I need to double-check it before submitting it first thing tomorrow morning.

Miss Yoshitaka takes forty minutes to finish, then tosses the documents on to my desk and leaves. I look at my watch and decide to take them home. I will look over them later. There is no overtime pay for work done at home, but this can't be helped.

~

Today is the final day of an antiques fair being held at a department store in Shinjuku ward. To my relief, I arrive one hour before closing time. Pottery, picture scrolls and various curios line the exhibition space. This kind of stock never sells out, which is why these fairs often look more like an exhibition than a sales event. Basically, antiques are a hard sell. But simply looking is enough for me, I think to myself, somewhat ironically, as my eyes linger longingly on an old Imari ceramic pot.

If I had my own shop, what kind of daily sales average would I need in order to remain profitable? After deductions for rent, utilities, office supplies and so on have been made. And there would be tax to pay as well. Once I begin running through the list in my mind, the only conclusion I can come to is that owning my own shop is a practical impossibility.

"Oy! Ryo? Is that you, Ryo?"

I turn around to see a middle-aged man with long, wavy permed hair standing behind me. He wears a shocking-pink jacket with a bright green floral pattern. It takes me a few seconds to recall the face.

"Mr. Nasuda?"

"The very same! Wow, you've got a good memory, Ryo!"

Mr. Nasuda had been a regular at Enmokuya. The only son of a real-estate agent, he had lived in a large three-story house on the same road and dabbled in various pursuits while also assisting his father. He liked to call himself "the prodigal son." In fact he was very fond of using that phrase. He was in his twenties when I knew him, and had aged in the past twenty years, predictably enough, but his liking for psychedelic fashion appeared unchanged and that was how I remembered him.

"You did a good job recognizing *me*, I should say."

"You haven't changed a bit, Ryo. Still as jumpy as ever."

The comment stings, but nostalgia wins out. It's coming back to me now—he was always like this.

"So, what do you do now, Ryo?"

"Oh, I'm just an ordinary office worker. What about you, Mr. Nasuda?"

"Oh, I'm just an ordinary prodigal son."

He hands me a business card case from the bag slung over his shoulder. It lists three job titles: "Design and renovation consultant," "Real-estate planner" and "Space consultant." I don't really understand it but I do get the gist that he is involved with various real-estate-related affairs.

"So, it's been years, hasn't it. It was a hell of a shock when Enmokuya closed all of a sudden."

"Yes, it really was."

"The cops paid a visit to our place, at the time. It was a big thing."

"The police?"

My heart begins thumping. All this time I was worried that Mr. Ebigawa had fallen ill, or become accidentally caught up in some kind of trouble.

"Apparently Mr. Ebigawa got into hot water and did a runner, owing big money."

My heart sinks. This was the thing I feared hearing most. More than sickness, or any other kind of trouble. Instantly my fantasy world feels besmirched.

"I never thought he was making much money," Mr. Nasuda says bitterly, "but he must've been desperate to do that. Disappearing like smoke—just like the name of the shop, hey."

This confirms all my fears that opening a shop is risky business—let alone an antique shop.

"You got a business card, Ryo?"

I pull one out and give it to Mr. Nasuda.

"How about that—you work for Kishimoto, the furniture maker. I know the company. If there's anything I can be of help with, get in contact. I do all kinds of things. Did you hear about the Rivera Showroom event? That was me—I organized it."

The event had been sponsored by a major interior-design company. It surprises me to learn he does proper business. But I can hardly say that, as it would sound rude. Being in the accounts department, I can't imagine having any reason to call on him for his services.

Mr. Nasuda's smartphone rings. He looks at the screen

and gives a small exclamation. "Let's have a drink some time," he says to me, then turns to his phone and begins talking into it as he leaves the room.

～

Next morning, I wait until no one else is around to speak to Miss Yoshitaka. The previous night I had checked the expenses report at home and verified that all the receipts and figures were in agreement. However, there was one receipt from Hosaka in Sales that bothers me. A coffee shop receipt with a prominent patch of dried correction fluid on it, and the number "1" written over it. If the amount visible underneath were correct, it would mean there is an erroneous entry in the expenses report, resulting in an excess claim of ten yen.

The original amount had been written in ballpoint pen. But the number written over the patch of dried correction fluid is in water-based ink, and even the handwriting is different. It was hard to imagine the coffee shop doing this. So was it Hosaka, or...?

"Miss Yoshitaka, regarding this," I say, pointing at the receipt.

Her face goes stony. "The numbers didn't match up, but only by just a bit," she says sullenly. "It wasn't worth the trouble asking Hosaka to redo it. What's the problem, anyway? It's only ten yen. The company won't collapse."

"It is not good practice."

"I'll pay it, then. Will that satisfy you?"

"No, it won't. That's not the point."

"Honestly, what's the fuss? Moaning about a measly ten yen won't do you any favors with girls."

"It's not a question of the amount!" My voice comes out so loud I surprise even myself.

Miss Yoshitaka's face turns red and she looks away. I don't think she'd expected I would yell at her.

"Jerk," she spits out, then grabs her things and leaves.

~

After that, I am on edge and cannot relax. The discussion hadn't gone well and it worries me that Miss Yoshitaka has disappeared. Where did she go? My boss, Mr. Taguchi, was having the day off, and is not around to help. Just as I am starting to think that perhaps I should report the incident to Personnel, they call me in.

The department head looks harried. "Miss Yoshitaka has lodged a complaint about power harassment by you. She's threatening to quit."

"She *what*!"

"She says you got in a rage when she accidentally

spilled correction fluid and rewrote the wrong number. She thought you were going to hit her, and was so afraid that she cried. Usually you're quiet, she says, but you change when the two of you are alone, according to her."

If anyone feels like crying, it's me. The injustice of it! I am nearly exploding with anger and disbelief. Accidentally spilled correction fluid? How dare she! It's true I spoke loudly, but to say I was about to hit her is outrageous—a false accusation.

However, there is no proof. Nothing I can do to prove my innocence.

"I'll look into the matter and discuss it with management," the department head tells me. He folds his arms and says darkly, "You do know the girl is the company president's niece, don't you? Taguchi is aware, but it might've been a good thing if he'd told you, too."

~

When I arrive home, Hina is waiting in my apartment with dinner ready. We are in the habit of spending Friday nights and all of Saturday together.

Over the plate of delicious beef stew she has cooked, I can't stop thinking about earlier. I am so fed up with my job. What am I doing there? Will I have to put up with this kind of thing until I retire? Unhappily biding my time in an office doing a job that doesn't excite me? And on top of everything, come home and not be able to stop thinking about work? There is never any escape from the petty frictions and irritations of dealing with other people, and having to come down on them about squaring the accounts and books. I might as well be at work right now. My job controls me. A job I don't want to be doing.

Nevertheless, it is a worry that it might be under threat. Much as I dislike it, I depend on my job and desperately want to protect it. It has always been that way and no doubt always will.

"Ryo, you seem a bit low." Hina looks at me with concern.

"Um, it's nothing. I'm busy at work, that's all. With bonus calculations and stuff," I tell her, glossing over the situation.

"Oh. You must be tired." She sets two glasses down on the table and then brings over a small bottle of wine. "I reached my monthly sales target for the online shop today. There were some fantastic reviews as well, and..."

Off she goes, chatting happily away.

I wish I could be like her. Only ever doing work that I like, and not having to deal with idiots, or worrying about financial insecurity, and whenever I make a tiny bit of money getting all excited and opening a bottle of wine to celebrate.

"I know it's online, but it really feels like having my own shop—it's such a good feeling. Hey, Ryo, when you have your antique shop—"

"Easy for you to say." I cut her off.

She flinches and looks shocked. I know I'm taking out my bad mood on her, but I can't help myself.

"I'm not like you, Hina. I can't take it easy having fun with my hobby. You don't have to worry if your online shop fails, or you don't sell anything!"

"It's not a hobby," Hina snaps.

The vehemence of her reply gives me a start, and I look at her.

"I'm not just fooling about playing shop, you know. Maybe it looks that way to you, but I'm not."

My head cools. Maybe I should apologize… But before I can say anything Hina has jumped smartly to her feet.

"I'm going home. You seem tired today, Ryo."

I sit there, fists clenched, not moving. Even when I hear the sound of the door shutting, I don't go after her. I've never felt so low.

~

With Hina gone, the weekend stretches out emptily before me. We rarely ever quarrel and I haven't felt so idiotic in a long time.

I flick through the TV channels but the raucous laughter from the variety shows is tinny and harsh in my ears, so I switch off. My eyes light on the book by my bed.

How Do Worms Work? Perhaps I can immerse myself in the wonders of nature instead. The more I read and the deeper I get into it, the more amazed and intrigued I am. And the strange thing is that surrendering myself to the wonders of a world apart from humans makes me begin to feel calmer. Similar to how I felt when I used to go to Enmokuya.

My estimation for the book grows. I like the way the questions—*Why are trees so big? Why can grass be mown? Why do some people talk to plants? Is it true that sunflower heads follow the sun?*—are laid out next to their answers. I like the texture of the pages—like a soft, bright, bleached white shirt, tightly packed between protective hard covers—and the way they open out and lie flat. The content is so clear and easy to understand, and the illustrations are fine and beautifully drawn. The whole volume exudes a sensibility that's quite different from the illustrated reference books I am accustomed to.

The third chapter is entitled "Below the Ground," with subsections such as *How do worms work? Where do roots go? How much of a plant is in its roots?* I find this chapter deeply fascinating. As I gaze at an illustration of a tree and its root system, with the earth the dividing line between what is above and what lies below, I am struck by a thought: most of the time we humans only look at the flowers or fruit of a plant, because we live aboveground. We switch our attention to belowground only when the roots have a particular interest for us, as in the case of sweet potatoes or carrots. Yet from a plant's perspective, aboveground and belowground are both equally important and in perfect balance.

Humans only see what suits them most, and make that their main focus, but for plants…

Both are main.

My mind jumps to the article about parallel careers where each job is complementary, neither is secondary. That's what Yasuhara had said.

Plants have work to do above and belowground, and their work in one area complements the other. Maybe it's the same with having an office job and running a store. Is that what Yasuhara is doing? What if I could do it too?

But how do I combine them? That is the question.

∾

The next afternoon I set out for Cats Now Books, catching a train from Shibuya to Sangenjaya, transferring to the Tokyu Setagaya Line and getting out at the tiny unmanned Nishi-Taishido station. I walk through the streets following the directions I have memorized. A light mid-December snow is falling. The area is residential and I see nothing that looks like a shop. Wondering if I am in the right place, I open up the map app on my phone to check. I continue to follow the narrow street until I reach a white house with a blue signboard under the eaves, with a yellow cat logo on it. A bay-window display is filled with books that all have cats on the covers.

I have found it.

When I open the door, a burst of warm air envelops me and I breathe a sigh of relief. A trim woman with bobbed hair sits behind a till, and the man in a blue checked shirt on the other side of a door with slats at the rear of the shop I take to be Yasuhara.

The area around the entrance has new publications, while secondhand books are displayed on the other side of the lattice door. I browse the shelves of new books until I feel slightly calmer.

"May I go in?" I ask the woman.

Removing my shoes as requested, I rub sanitizer on my hands and open the lattice door. This is where the cats are. The brown mackerel tabby that looks exactly like the felt mascot Ms. Komachi gave me is curled up on a cushion. Another tabby and a black cat stroll nonchalantly between the shelves.

"Welcome." Yasuhara turns from a customer to greet

me. He has a pleasant, mellow voice and a mild demeanor, but is more intellectual-looking than I expected from his photo.

In the middle of the secondhand book area there is a table with a small drinks menu on it. I read it three times over, trying to prolong my time in here as much as possible. "Excuse me—could I order a coffee, please?"

"Yes. Hot or iced?"

"Hot," I reply.

Yasuhara makes eye contact with the woman on the other side of the lattice door, who comes in and goes through to the kitchen.

A cat wanders around my feet. A tabby, with a white stomach and paws. The cats all seem to be extremely relaxed and at home.

The woman brings me my coffee and returns to the till. I gaze around me at the books on display. It feels good to be sitting here drinking coffee and watching cats, surrounded by books. I feel content and relaxed. If I left now, my visit would still have been perfectly satisfactory.

A mackerel tabby wearing an orange collar climbs silently to perch high up. This is the same cat that had been asleep on the cushion before. It settles and waves its tail. Our eyes meet. *Aren't you here for a reason? Don't you want to know what it's like to achieve your dream?* I feel as if the cat is speaking to me. I gather myself to speak.

When the other customer moves away toward the till, I put down my coffee and stand up. "Um, excuse me…"

Yasuhara turns.

"I came today because I read an article by the librarian at Hatori Community House."

He smiles. "Ah, yes. Ms. Komachi kindly recommended us. Thank you for coming."

"Um, actually I'm thinking about opening a shop too."

It had been my intention to ease into the topic gradually but the words spill out in a rush. Drat. Now Yasuhara will think I am a naive young man looking for a quick fix to solve all his problems, and feel offended.

I needn't have worried. His face lights up. "A bookshop?"

"No, antiques."

He nods, looking interested.

"I also read some of the interviews you did online," I continue. "I'd never heard of a parallel career before. You work for a company during the week, don't you?"

"That's right."

"Do you mind if I ask some questions. My name is Ryo Urase, by the way. I work for a furniture manufacturer, in the accounts department."

"Happy to. We won't get many customers in this cold weather anyway."

Yasuhara sits down on a stool and signals for me to take one next to it. I sit down, still not knowing where to start. But before I can put my thoughts in order, the words just tumble out.

"Isn't it hard work to manage a shop and work for a company at the same time? Don't you ever find that either gets too much?"

Yasuhara laughs lightly. "No, I don't. If anything, it's doing both that makes me feel like neither is ever too much of a burden."

The mackerel tabby strolls over and jumps on to Yasuhara's lap.

"Before I had this place, all I ever used to think about was quitting my office job, but now that job is what gives me the means to enjoy running this bookshop. If the bookshop was all I did, however, then I'd have to spend a lot more time thinking about sales strategies and so on. Which would be far more demanding. And I don't really want that."

He strokes the cat along its body. "I believe that a job secures you a place in society. So if you have a parallel career, you can have two places. With neither a side business."

A place in society. Having a presence in two fields and functioning in both. Aboveground and belowground— this image of the plant world is at the back of my mind as I ask, "You said in the interview that neither was secondary to the other."

"Yes."

"But do you make as much money from the bookshop as working for a company?"

The instant I say this, I regret it. But Yasuhara brushes it off with a laugh.

"I don't mean secondary in that sense. To put it bluntly, I get more from the shop in terms of mental and emotional satisfaction than I do in monetary profit. Though, of course, I am interested in increasing sales to keep the business afloat."

The concept of being mentally and emotionally fulfilled from doing the thing I like is something I can relate to. But if both jobs are main, wouldn't that mean working constantly, seven days a week? I wonder if Yasuhara ever feels like slacking off, taking a break or going away? I choose my words carefully.

"But if you work in both an office and a shop, you'd never be able to go away anywhere, would you?"

"That's true," he says with a nod, in a tone that suggests this is something he is used to being asked. "But I meet people here I wouldn't otherwise and have some really interesting encounters. It's like traveling to lots of different places every day. I might be in here all the time and never go out, but I get as much enjoyment out of it as I would from, say, a pastime like fishing."

Does he, indeed. What kind of experiences has he had? Who has he met here that can cause him to speak with such conviction? Owning a shop might have more advantages than I imagined. But whatever they are, I suspect that Yasuhara himself is a key factor. He seems smart, knowledgeable, discerning, well connected and having the courage of his convictions—not like me.

"I don't have anything. Not enough time, money or courage. I always think that one day I'll do it, but I never do. I don't have what it takes to get started."

Yasuhara stares at the mackerel tabby in silence. I worry that I have worn out my welcome with all my negativity. Then he turns to face me and I see he is smiling.

"The moment you say 'don't,' you're done for."

"Excuse me?"

"You have to turn that 'don't' into a goal."

Turn "don't" into a "goal"? What's that supposed to mean? Find the funds, make the time, pluck up the courage? I see him observing me as I struggle to voice these thoughts aloud.

"I don't like being around people, you know," he says, and gives a wry smile.

Another extraordinary statement! And not one I would expect to hear from someone I've only just met. Not to mention someone with a customer service business, who happens to be speaking most kindly to me at this very moment.

"But there came a time when I thought I ought to make an effort, and listen to what other people might have to say. Once I started to show my face here and there, I had encounters that led to all sorts of opportunities and connections."

The mackerel tabby jumps down from Yasuhara's lap. It ambles over to the black cat and put its face up close, as if there is something it simply must convey.

"Everybody is connected. And any one of their connections could be the start of a network that branches in many directions. If you wait for the right time to make connections, it might never happen, but if you show your face around, talk to people and see enough to give you the confidence that things could work out, then 'one day' might turn into 'tomorrow.'"

Looking at the cats, he adds, "Timing is all-important. Don't let the right moment slip by."

It sounds very much as if he is talking about fate. For someone who seems to be such a realist, they are weighty words. I look at him enviously.

"But you're doing what you want to be doing, now, aren't you?" I ask. "You've achieved your dream?"

Yasuhara tips his head to one side. "I don't think of this as the dream."

"But..."

"If all I wanted was to be surrounded by cats and books and beer, I wouldn't need a bookshop to achieve that. When I opened this place, that didn't mean that I got what I wanted and that was the end of it. Now I have the shop there are things still to do. Things that can't be expressed in numbers."

This throws me. Here he is in the perfect setup, and still looking for other things to do? But when I look at his face and see the light in his eyes, it makes perfect sense. I could see how this might be the true goal of the dream.

Yasuhara places his hands on the table in front of him and clasps them together. "Ryo, let me ask, why do you want to open an antique shop? Not just to be surrounded by antiques, surely—why open a shop?"

I look at the ground. This is the question that will lead me to the path I ought to take, and in truth I already know the answer.

"I'll have a good think about it."

At some point, the mackerel tabby at my feet has nestled itself against my shins. I get down from the stool to pat it.

"Ryo, do you plan to open a shop by yourself?"

In my mind I see Hina's face. If only she would do it with me, I would be so happy. But that…

"It's hard work on your own," says Yasuhara. "You need someone else there—a partner, family member or friend—someone to discuss things with and let off steam. If you don't have a partner to share the mental stress, it's exhausting."

Yasuhara looks over in the direction of the lattice door, and the woman behind the till.

I get it. "She's your partner, isn't she?"

"Misumi, my wife."

"What did she say when you told her you wanted to open a shop?"

Yasuhara looks away. "She didn't…say anything." Then he turns toward me with a gentle smile, and with an expression I have not seen on his face before. "She said nothing, and went along with it. I'm forever grateful to her."

≈

The next day, Sunday, I return to the Hatori Community House on my own. Ostensibly to return the library book, but there is somebody I want to see. After handing the book to Nozomi, I go over to the reference corner.

"Ms. Komachi. I paid a visit to Cats Now Books."

Her eyes open just the tiniest bit wider and she gives a satisfied smile.

"The Yasuharas send you their regards."

"Ah, Misumi is an old friend. We used to work at the same library. How is she?"

"She seems fine. They're a nice couple," I say, and take the felt cat mascot from my bag. "You pointed me at that shop, didn't you. I want to thank you. I'm going to try and get started on doing something now, not just wait for one day to come along."

Her head tilts ever so slightly to one side. "But you're already doing something."

I swallow.

"I didn't send you there," she continues. "You noticed that shop by yourself. You decided to go there, and you made the effort to meet Yasuhara. You've already begun."

Then she twists her neck around with a clicking sound. The felt cat sitting on the palm of my hand stares at me with eyes that looks as if they might spring to life at any moment.

~

There is one more person I must see. After leaving the Community House, I head for Hina's place. I put my hand in my pocket and gently rub the sheep spoon that I'd put in there for good luck.

Before leaving home that morning, I had phoned Hina to apologize for Friday and to ask to meet. She told me to come over as her parents were away. When I arrive at her house, I ring the doorbell and she answers the door immediately.

"Come in."

I enter and follow her up the stairs to her room. Tools and pieces of sea glass are scattered across her desk. She must be in the middle of making accessories.

"I'm sorry about the other day," I say, repeating what I'd already said that morning. My limited range of self-expression is disappointing.

Hina bursts out laughing. "You already said that."

Her smile is my salvation. From my bag I pull out a bottle of wine and two glasses—the same bottle she had brought to my apartment. She looks surprised as I open it and pour two glasses.

"Congratulations on meeting your target."

"Thank you," she says, with a self-conscious nod of acknowledgment. "Cheers."

Wine sloshes up the sides of the glasses as we clink them together in a toast.

"You're amazing, Hina. Not just because you achieved

your sales target, but because you make your own path—that's really impressive."

Hina flashes me a quick smile and picks up a piece of sea glass from her desk.

"You know, some people believe that the future owner of a handmade object is already decided before it's made. It sounds corny, I know, but that's kind of how I feel."

"Uh-huh."

"When I make a piece of jewelry, I think about the person who might wear or use it. I don't see their face or anything like that; it's more that I feel a connection with the unknown person who will own it. So when I'm working on a piece of sea glass and think about it passing through my hands on a long, long journey in time and space to the person it's meant to be with, well, that just makes me feel super happy."

I can really relate to that.

I feel the weight of my own treasured object in my pocket. Enmokuya may not exist anymore, but it is the place where I found my spoon. A spoon that could have been used by an aristocratic lady for her afternoon tea, or a mother to feed her young son, who in turn treasured it long after he grew up, or a favorite spoon in a family of three sisters. I might even have used it when I was little. It has gone from hand to hand to end up with me. Enmokuya brought me together with my spoon.

I want to do the same. I want to bring people together with the objects they are meant to meet. Objects that are meant to be passed on, forever, belonging to different people at different points in time. I want to be the intermediary for such encounters. To provide a space where they might occur. This is the biggest reason I want my own shop.

~

"Hina, I have something to show you." I pull a thin file from my bag and open it up in front of her. It is a budget spreadsheet I made the night before. An estimate of how much I need to set up an antique shop and run it.

I calculated the up-front costs of acquiring a property, renovating the interior, installing air conditioning, fixtures and furnishings and buying equipment. And ongoing costs for rent, utilities, office supplies and stock once it opens. Then I calculated the average daily takings required to maintain the shop. I racked my brains and drew on everything I knew about accounting in order to come up with this blueprint.

"I'm going to prepare to open a shop. But I won't quit the company. I plan to keep my job and run a shop at the same time."

Hina claps both hands over her mouth and looks at me with wide, dancing eyes.

"Ryo, this is fantastic! It's a wonderful idea! You are so amazing, being able to make something like this happen!"

So... So...will you help me? I bite back the words I'd planned to say as a marriage proposal. After all, I can't be sure it will work out, and if we were to marry before opening the shop, it might make more work for Hina— no, take that back, it's *certain* to make more work—so it would be better to wait until I've got the whole thing running smoothly, and learned the knack of doing both jobs at the same time, then I'll—oh, damn. There I go again, saying *one day*.

I feel deflated. I am not like Yasuhara. I can never be the kind of man a woman will follow without question.

I am fast chickening out when Hina breaks through these thoughts. "Ryo, let's get married. The sooner the better."

Just like that.

For a second, I am speechless. I splutter, "Uh...uh," because I remember Mr. Ebigawa from Enmokuya who ended up becoming a matter for the police. "But what if it doesn't work out and the shop fails..." I protest.

"If it fails? Is that not allowed?" Hina demands.

Oh. My thoughts do a swift about-turn. With astonishment, I realize that it *is* allowed. The reason for the law's interest in Mr. Ebigawa was his failure to pay off his debts after disappearing. Not because the shop failed.

"Say we did have to close the shop, it's not going to harm anybody, is it? It just doesn't look good, that's all. I have no use for stupid pride, Ryo. Besides, don't you think it would be so much easier to do this together as a couple rather than have to employ a stranger to help?"

Did she say *Do this together...*? Yes, that's what she said.

Suddenly, I feel braver. Now I get what Yasuhara must have felt too. When he told me that Misumi went along with it, he must have meant it in the sense that they did it together. There is no main job and secondary job. Both are equally important. That could be true for a couple, too.

Hina is staring off into space, mulling over something. "If we go ahead with this, there's a ton of things to do, Ryo. You have to go to the police for a start."

"The police?"

"Yes, of course. To get an antique dealer's license. You have to lodge the application with the police."

I laugh. She is right. All roads lead to the police.

Hina taps one finger against her chin, deep in thought. "But we should get started on crowdfunding before anything."

Yasuhara had also mentioned crowdfunding in his interviews. To hear Hina propose such a thing is startling.

"Is that easy for amateurs?" I ask.

She rolls her eyes. "Ryo, crowdfunding is what amateurs *do*." Then, leaning in close, she asks, "Ryo, dear, have you ever thought about what makes the world go round?"

"Er...er, love, I guess."

"Oh, that's priceless!" she cries. "You never cease to amaze me, Ryo, but that's what I love about you. I believe it is trust," she adds.

"Trust?"

"Yes, trust. Anything you do—borrowing money from a bank, commissioning a piece of work, sending or receiving a parcel, making a plan with friends, ordering food at a restaurant—all those things can only happen because of mutual trust on both sides."

I stare at her as the words roll off her tongue. I always knew that Hina was far more information-savvy than I am—she's always alert to what's going on and forever weighing things up—but now I see what a go-getter she really is.

But then, if I'm absolutely honest with myself, I simply might have been pretending not to notice all along. Deep down I've always known: Hina's head is not in the clouds. It is only my stupid pride at being a man, and ten years older than her, which got in the way of my acknowledging her for who she truly is.

"If money is your only object, then crowdfunding can

be a lot of trouble for nothing, because you don't know if you'll raise enough to start a business. But it's a brilliant method of PR. That's what makes it really worth doing. It's a way for you to show people your passion, and earn their trust. If anything, it's the people who have no business experience but are totally sincere who get the best response. And once you open a shop, everybody who's been supporting you online is happy to come and see it. That's the great thing."

My heart begins beating faster. Though it is still only hypothetical, I can envisage a picture of us, together, at the center of this dream, one that now seems totally real and possible.

"You know, Hina, I think I might be getting excited about this," I tell her, putting my hands to my chest for emphasis.

She grabs my arms joyfully. "That's what I wanted to see! Choosing to do something because it excites you is the best reason of all. I just know it."

My glance falls on a small glass bottle on a corner of Hina's desk and I remember what Yasuhara had said. "The important thing…"

Inside that glass bottle, which Hina clearly treasures, is the piece of red sea glass I gave her that day we met on the beach. All of a sudden I feel confident. It will be all right. I can do it.

~

The next day, Monday, I am summoned to the company president's office. What was my punishment to be? Salary cut, demotion or, in the worst case, getting fired? The abrupt termination of my office job would be no laughing matter with my eyes now set on a parallel career.

Instead, the president greets me with an apology. "Miya's been causing trouble. I'm sorry."

Miya? He is talking about Miss Yoshitaka.

"Personnel reported the incident to me on Friday. I asked Miya what happened and she repeated the same story, but then I saw Taguchi at golf on Saturday."

"Mr. Taguchi…"

"When I told him, he was furious. You'd never do anything like that in a million years, according to him. He told me that there is nobody more sincere and trustworthy than you; even all the other departments think so."

I am flabbergasted. Mr. Taguchi said that? Even knowing that Miss Yoshitaka was the president's niece?

"I was quite taken aback, I can tell you. I've known Taguchi a long time but never has he spoken to me in that manner. So then I had another chat with Miya and she admitted it was her fault."

It is just as Hina said. The president trusts Taguchi, Taguchi trusts me. Trust makes the world go round.

~

Miss Yoshitaka is absent from work that day but turns up again the next, looking nonchalant. She comes to stand in front of me and says sullenly, "I'm sorry." Then, without meeting my eye, bows deep in apology.

"It's okay…let's get back to work now," I say to the back of her head. And that is the end of it.

Later, when she is away on an errand, Mr. Taguchi says, "Urase, you let her off too easily. She's probably giving you the finger in her head."

I smile wryly. "Well, at least she didn't quit and run away. She turned up to work again, so I'm fairly sure she feels guilty. That's why I've decided to trust her from now on."

Mr. Taguchi pulls a skeptical face.

I hand him three pieces of paper. "This is a trouble-shooting manual I put together for the new software. I collated sections that you might have problems with."

"What?" He stares at the manual I made for him. "This is great. An enormous help," he says with a nod of thanks.

"I think it will help us both be more efficient."

Yes. Now he won't have any excuse to interrupt his own work to ask me what to do, or repeat the same question over and over. This manual is one step of preparation for my parallel career. The first thing I need to do is streamline my work in the office. No more unnecessary overtime.

"Urase, there's something different about you today," Mr. Taguchi says teasingly. "Since you're in a such a good mood, how about going out for a drink?"

"Sorry, but I have to leave on time today."

Tonight I am seeing Mr. Nasuda, who is going to teach me about shop locations, real-estate companies, interior furnishings, and so on. Things I need to know to open a shop. Hina is also going to contact the minerals lecturer, Mr. Mogi, for more information on buying supplies. Together we are setting ourselves in motion, pulling on the invisible threads of our connections. There are so many things to do, but I won't make the excuse that I have no time anymore. Instead, I will think about what I can do with the time I have.

One day is going to become *tomorrow*.

3

Natsumi, 40, former magazine editor

We all come to understand at some point in our lives that there is no Santa Claus. But the reason Santa Claus remains an integral part of Christmas celebrations is not for the sake of small children. It is because grown-ups who were once children themselves continue to hold the truth of Santa Claus in their hearts even after they become adults, and they live in that belief.

How many times have I read these words? More than I can count. I sometimes I carry this book about with me like a talisman—a colorful array of sticky notes poking out from its pages, contrasting starkly with the whiteness within. Something else that appeals to me.

This morning I turned the calendar over to December. Christmas is nearly upon us. What shall I give Futaba this year, I wonder? Oh, Santa has such fun problems to solve!

December sunshine warms my skin as I think back over the year. It's been three months now since the events of the summer. I gaze out of the window. Above, the waxing moon is still faintly visible in a winter-blue midday sky.

August. The summer holidays were over and the office was back to operating normally. I was working for a publisher called Banyusha, in their information resources department. My job was to archive all their digital and print publications, retrieve data for employees upon request, and seek various permissions when required. I also wrote company profiles for the website and other PR material for external use.

There were six of us in Information Resources, all men apart from myself, ranging from early to late middle age. They were never very communicative with me and after two years I still didn't feel at ease there.

Before transferring to Information Resources, I had worked as an editor in charge of producing a general-interest magazine called *Mila*, for young women. I had spent thirteen years of my working life devoting myself to *Mila*. Then I became pregnant, which was a surprise but not unexpected. By then I was thirty-seven and conscious of time passing, so it was welcome news. I thought it would be good to have a baby at that age to minimize any future risk to my health, and planned to return to work as soon as possible to minimize the risk to my career.

I can't deny that in the beginning I did go slightly overboard in downplaying my pregnancy. I told no one apart from the editor in chief until I was past the twelve-week mark, because I didn't want to be treated differently. I put up with morning sickness in secret, and fought off the overpowering sleepiness brought on by hormonal changes, with large quantities of mint chewing gum. Once my belly became too big to hide and I had made the announcement, I still desperately tried to make sure that nobody would have a problem working with me because I was pregnant.

I worked right up until my last month and gave birth in January. Then I returned to work four months later, despite being entitled to fourteen months of maternity leave. I was determined to get back as soon as possible, even if that meant putting three-month-old Futaba into daycare. I did have reservations, but felt impelled to get back to my desk as soon as I was able.

On my first day back at work, naturally I went straight to the *Mila* section. My colleagues greeted me warmly, but I was conscious of an underlying note of awkwardness that made me wonder. When the editor in chief called me in, I discovered why. "Ms. Sakitani, may I have a word?" he said, ushering me into a conference room. There, I was abruptly informed of my transfer to Information Resources.

"Why?" I eventually managed to croak out shakily.

"Because it's too hard to work as an editor with a baby," he replied, as if it was a matter of no great import.

"But I…"

I was seething with an anger that I couldn't put into words.

Why, why, why? All through maternity leave I had read *Mila* cover to cover every month, come up with ideas and plans for future features and studied the reference materials, all on the assumption that I was returning to my position. I'd kept myself prepared and ready to get on top of the work the moment I was back.

It had never even occurred to me that I might lose my position. Everything I had built up over thirteen years at *Mila*—what had it all been for? Had my contribution and impact been of such little consequence that they weren't prepared to wait for me?

"HR also agree with me that we want to make it easy for you to work nine to five," the editor in chief said in a consoling tone.

"I'm fine, I can handle work and a baby," I jumped in. "My husband and I talked it over. We'll share the work between us, not to mention the various babysitters I have lined up for when I need to do overtime or have meetings at night—"

"The decision's been made. No need to push yourself," he rebuffed me wearily. "Information Resources will be far easier on you."

That was probably the first time I ever knew true despair. No doubt the company believed their decision was for the best. But I didn't want it to be easy. To me it was like being told I was no longer useful. I felt as if I had been pushed into a deep, black hole.

No other women on the staff at Banyusha had children, so there was no precedent. Had I been too optimistic in thinking that I might be the one to set it?

Two years went by. I often thought about looking for a new position with another magazine. From a practical point of view, however, things at home had not fallen into place as I had hoped. Coordinating responsibilities with my husband, Shuji, was not going smoothly, and I was discovering that where a child was concerned, you never knew what was going to happen. I had far less freedom than I expected and found it difficult to make plans.

It pains me to admit this, but the editor in chief might have been right. It would have been difficult for me to work in the same way as I had before. In the end, I decided that the best course was to bide my time in Information Resources until Futaba was bigger.

~

The hands on the wall clock showed it was just after five. Being careful not to make any noise, I slung my bag over my shoulder and stood up from my desk to leave. Everybody else had their heads down, still deep in their work. I knew I was doing nothing wrong but felt guilty nonetheless leaving at this hour.

I hadn't been able to get Futaba into the daycare center nearest our home as there was a long waiting list. In order to be ready for my planned return to work, I'd had to settle instead for another place a short walk from the next station down. Which meant it was also further from the office. Even when I left at five, it was tight. If I missed just one train, I could not get another connection in time and would run late. The sight of Futaba waiting alone after all the other children had gone always wrung my heart.

It was a fast seven-minute walk to the station. The first three minutes of that I spent feeling guilty about my colleagues still at work, the last four about Futaba waiting for me. *I'm sorry, I'm sorry* kept replaying in my mind as I passed through the ticket gate. Shuji would no doubt be late again tonight. I stood in the train gazing blankly out at the scenery rushing by. I could never get used to leaving work while it was still daylight.

~

Shuji works for an events company, and these days he seems to have to go on a lot more business trips and work overtime. On the train, I thought back to how yesterday he had told me that he was going away on a business trip over the weekend. Maybe it really was a last-minute arrangement, but I still couldn't help wishing I'd known earlier. There are so many small jobs that demand my attention every day. Daycare, for instance, does not simply involve taking Futaba there and picking her up. Every evening I have to check her diary for notes from the staff, get her things ready for the next day, and prepare for the various events held throughout the year. At the weekend I do the jobs that I don't have time for during the week, like airing futons, cleaning the bathroom and replenishing the contents of the fridge.

But it's not as if I absolutely have to do these. When Shuji isn't home, it doesn't matter if the bathroom is a bit grungy and I can make do with anything for meals. What I find most trying is looking forward to sharing the housework and childcare at the weekend, but ending up having to do it all myself.

Shuji is more of a doting parent than I am. He's never objected to changing diapers, and when Futaba started on solids, he took it upon himself to search for recipes online and make them himself. Mostly, however, it shows in the way he looks at her with such love and tenderness.

When I'm finding things hard, just him being there makes me feel so much better. I feel trapped being alone with a toddler who I can't take my eyes off for a second. Of course I love Futaba—that goes without saying—but that emotion and the suffocating feeling that comes as a result of being closeted up alone with a toddler are two completely different issues.

~

After seeing Shuji off early the next morning, I was about to go back to bed when Futaba woke up. I don't know why she always has to wake up early at weekends.

We ate breakfast and then she proceeded to pull every single toy out of her toy box to play with. I seized the opportunity to hang out the washing. Futaba's sheets take up most of the space on the clothes-drying pole on the balcony, so I have to cram all the hangers close together to fit everything in.

The daycare center has very specific requirements about the futon cover. It must be the type with a zipper, and every Friday afternoon when I collect Futaba I remove the cover from her futon, then return it, washed, on Monday morning. It's a lot of effort at the start of the week, but when I mentioned this to Shuji, he merely said, "Oh, is that so." Recalling the conversation filled me with annoyance all over again.

I returned to the living room to find Futaba glued to the television watching an anime, with her toys spread all over the floor.

"Fu-*chan*, if you're finished with your toys let's put them away."

"No."

"I'll throw them away if you leave them out."

"No! No throw away!"

"Well, tidy them up."

"No."

She's going through a defiant phase. All the books say that this is typical of the terrible twos. It's a developmental stage and the best response is to be patient and not scold. Suppressing my own childish irritation, I picked my way through the scattered toys to the kitchen.

Futaba's sippy cup was still in the sink where I had left it last night. It has a straw that pops out when you open the lid and is such a nuisance to clean. I disassembled it and put the rubber rings in bleach to soak off stains and disinfect them. Yet another of my weekend chores, one of the many small fiddly tasks that eat up more time than one would expect. This is why I never have time to unwind at the weekend.

Patience. If only I could buy it, I'd place a bulk order. I sighed. Maybe I wasn't cut out for having children. I was expecting to cope better than this. The thought of two whole days alone with Futaba was daunting.

Maybe we could go to the park? I wouldn't mind if we were lucky enough to have it to ourselves, but when there are gaggles of other mothers around, I get so shy and self-conscious that more often than not Futaba and I end up simply wandering about. On second thoughts, the park might not be the best plan after all.

Where else could we go that would allow us to pass the time pleasantly without raising my stress levels? Excursions to the aquarium and zoo are major undertakings, while going to the city library involves catching a bus, which has reduced services at weekends.

I remembered the daycare director once saying that the library in Hatori Community House, a small community center next to the local elementary school, has an area where little kids can play. I hadn't paid much attention at the time as I'd been on the point of leaving, but a quick search on my smartphone revealed that this

Community House was quite an impressive facility and did indeed have an area called Kids' Space. It has Western-and Japanese-style meeting rooms, and also runs courses for adults, apparently.

The school is where Futaba will eventually go and since it is only ten minutes' walk from home, I decided it would be a nice stroll along with an opportunity to familiarize myself with the area, albeit somewhat prematurely.

"Fu-*chan*, shall we go out?"

Futaba jumped to her feet from her position in front of the television. Thank goodness she didn't say no.

～

Futaba skipped along the sidewalk beside me with her hand in mine. Her tiny head, covered with a straw hat, bobbing along beside me.

"Fu-*chan* wear sogs," she said, looking happily up at me.

I smiled. *Sogs.* She was talking about her favorite socks with cats on them. She's so cute when she says this, even if I do say so myself.

We passed by the school front gate and followed the perimeter fence around until reaching a signboard with an arrow and the words "Community House this way" that pointed us down a narrow street to a solid-looking white building. At reception I wrote our names, purpose of visit and time of arrival in a log on the front desk, and we went in.

The library was on the ground floor at the rear of the building. When we entered, I immediately noted the Kids' Space on the right at the back. Low bookshelves enclosed an area covered by a soft rubber floor mat, set with tiny tables that had rounded corners. To my relief, nobody else was there.

Futaba and I removed our shoes and sat down. It was soothing to be surrounded by picture books and I pulled out several at random that caught my eye. I ran my eyes over the names of the publishing companies: Sky Sounds, Maple, Star Clouds. Children's publishing companies have such lovely, warm names.

Futaba began peeling off her socks. Why, when just a short time before she had been so happy to be wearing them?

"Fu-*chan*, are you hot?"

"Befut. Befut Jerop."

"Barefoot Jerop?"

I can interpret most things Futaba says, but some defeat me. She began wandering around the shelves. I rolled up her socks and stored them in my voluminous bag.

Suddenly a young woman with a ponytail bobbed up over the shelves to peer at us.

"Maybe she means Gerob?"

She wore a navy-blue apron that looked like a staff uniform and was holding several books. The name tag hanging from her neck read "Nozomi Morinaga."

"It's a popular series called *Barefoot Gerob*. A picture book about a centipede," Nozomi said, with a smile as fresh as new green buds.

"Eww, a centipede?"

Nozomi giggled as she removed her shoes and entered the space. She placed the books on one of the low tables, then deftly extracted a volume from the shelves and handed it to Futaba.

"Jerop!" Futaba whooped, and jumped on it.

She must have known it from daycare. When she opened the book, I saw a picture of a centipede trying to put shoes on its numerous feet. Half were barefoot while the other half were clad in an assortment of different footwear. It was a strange, almost grotesque picture, hardly what I'd call cute.

Nozomi looked at it. "Adults tend to think Gerob is a gross character, but children love it. The book has pictures of flies and cockroaches in it too. They're drawn with real affection. It's a lovely book, I think, because it's written from a child's perspective. Children don't have the prejudices that adults do about insects we usually regard as pests."

A true professional, I noted admiringly with a nod of agreement.

"Can we borrow this book?"

"Yes, if you live in the ward. If you're looking for anything else, the librarian is over there."

Nozomi pointed to the opposite side of the room at the rear. A partition blocked the view, but a sign labeled "Reference" dangled from the ceiling.

"I thought you were the librarian," I said.

Nozomi blushed and waved her hands in the air dismissively. "Oh no, I'm still a trainee. I only just graduated from high school, so I need three years of practical work experience to become a librarian. I'm still in my first year, so I have a way to go. I must keep trying."

Her dazzling youth and those big moist eyes made me quite dizzy. I was moved by her determination. She reminded me of myself, and my own considerable effort to find the perfect job and company when I graduated from college.

I had ambitions to work in publishing and create books. I was already a *Mila* fan when I joined Banyusha and was thrilled, of course, to be assigned to work on it. Five years ago, *Mila* ran a serialized novel by famous author Mizue Kanata that became a popular hit, and I was the one who had made it happen.

Madam Mizue was seventy at the time, an age that in

the editor in chief's opinion disqualified her from writing for a magazine aimed at young women. He also flatly rejected the idea of a serialized novel in a general-interest magazine such as ours. An essay would be more appropriate, according to him. But I believed in the power of Madam Mizue's writing to reach our readers. I was convinced that the strong message of hope that runs through her historical and literary novels would resonate with women in their twenties. And I was positive that if she chose a setting and style with *Mila* readers in mind, they would be hooked and buy the magazine every month in anticipation of the next instalment.

My next strategy was to tackle the managing director, who also poured cold water on the idea. "But if she can be persuaded, give it a try," he said, not believing for a moment that such a distinguished author would even consider it.

Thus I began a heated campaign of persuasion. At first, Madam Mizue rejected me on the grounds that a monthly serial was too much hard work at her age. But I was persistent and kept putting my case to her. I pleaded that this was an opportunity to convey the optimism and passion for life that permeated her novels to an audience of young women striving to live full lives. I promised her complete support if she would agree.

On my fifth attempt, she finally did. "I'm curious

to see what kind of story I can produce while working with you, Ms. Sakitani," she told me. The title of the serial novel that she subsequently penned was *The Pink Plane Tree*, about the relationship, neither friendship nor rivalry, between two girls with widely differing characters. It quickly became a centerpiece in *Mila* and sales rose. The serial ended up becoming hugely popular and ran for eighteen months. At its conclusion, management decided to publish it in book format as well. Banyusha, however, has no fiction department, therefore it became my job to oversee its production as a novel and secure distribution with bookstores. I did all that on top of my usual editing duties, which made it my busiest period ever since starting at the company. But every day was so fulfilling I felt alive and trembling with joy.

The book went on to win the Bookshelf Prize, a major annual literary award, which naturally everybody at work was jubilant about. It was unheard of for a magazine publisher like Banyusha to be in the limelight for literature. The managing director even stopped me in the corridor to hint at a promotion to deputy editor in chief.

Not long after that, I discovered I was pregnant. I wasn't without qualms at being away from my desk for a time, but was confident in the contribution I had made to the company. I loved my job, I had a relationship of trust with Madam Mizue, and when I returned to work

I planned to forge ahead and achieve even more. For me, the job of editor was all about reaping the fruits of a long, careful accumulation of effort.

But it was not to be. All my experience and effort were for nothing. If I had known I would not be returning to *Mila*, I would have devoted more of my attention to Futaba while on maternity leave instead of filling my head with plans for work. In the precious little time I had to myself while she slept, I would have rested too, or watched Korean dramas, or taken up a hobby instead of wasting time and energy on coming up with new feature ideas for *Mila* and doing all the background research that entailed.

I found myself now in a position where I was neither fully satisfied with my job nor with motherhood, yet I had to spend every moment juggling both.

Every day felt like I was merely going around in circles, marking out time, day after day, and going nowhere.

~

Futaba sat plonked on the floor with a picture book open in front of her.

"Fu-*chan*, shall we go and ask the lady about more fun books?"

I knew she could hear me but was too engrossed in Gerob to even say no.

"I'll watch Fu-*chan*," Nozomi said. "Please, you go and see her."

"Oh, but I—"

"Really, it's fine. There's nobody else in here now."

Taking her at her word, I put my shoes back on. If I could find a few entertaining picture books for Futaba here, I might manage to make it through the weekend.

The reference corner was separated off by a partition that doubled as a noticeboard. As I approached, I glanced over to the other side and my feet came to a sudden stop. Behind the counter sat a large, pale woman of indeterminate age, but if pressed to say, I might put her in her fifties. She wore a long-sleeved white shirt that was not a garment one would find on the racks of any ordinary clothes shop; it had to be either custom-made or a special order from overseas. But with her ivory apron and smooth, unblemished, pure white skin, she reminded me of the Disney Baymax character.

The librarian sat behind the counter, looking down solemnly with an expression of deep concentration, engaged in a delicate task of some kind. I approached, curious to know what was occupying her, and saw to my surprise that she was jabbing a needle into what looked like a ball of wool resting on a sponge mat.

She was felting. I recognized it because we had covered it in a handicraft feature at *Mila*, although it had not been my project. Stabbing at strands of wool with a felting needle creates the shape. It seemed incongruous for such a large person to be engaged in producing so tiny an object. I stared at her hands with the sense of watching an anime. She appeared to be making some kind of mascot.

I recognized the dark-orange box next to her as Honeydome cookies made by Kuremiyado, an old established company known for its Western-style confectionery. They're delicious. A half-moon-shaped cookie with a soft, honey-flavored center. We used to give them to artists who contributed to *Mila*. The thought of the librarian liking them, too, made me feel a bond with her.

The hands stopped moving. When the librarian lifted her head and looked at me, I felt like shrinking.

"Er, I beg your pardon…"

An apology wasn't called for, but I withered under that gaze and was edging my way out when she spoke.

"What are you looking for?"

Her voice was flat and low pitched. Though neither kind nor friendly, it was reassuring nonetheless. I felt gently enfolded by those few words that imparted an instant impression of a big heart I felt I could trust, body and soul.

What am I looking for? I could give many answers: my future path in life, a way of releasing my frustrations, the patience to raise a child, etcetera. But where would I find them? And besides, this was not a counseling room.

"Picture books," I answered simply.

The name tag on the librarian's chest read Sayuri Komachi." How sweet: small-town Sayuri, Ms. Komachi the librarian.

Ms. Komachi opened the lid of the Honeydome box and put away her needle. Apparently it was an empty box used for her sewing tools.

"Picture books," she repeated evenly. "We do have a lot of those."

"Something suitable for my two-year-old daughter. She's fond of *Barefoot Gerob.*"

Ms. Komachi swayed and made a rumbling sound. "Aaah, a popular favorite," she said.

"It does appear so. Though I can't say I understand what children like," I lamented.

She tilted her head slightly to one side and looked at me searchingly. Her hair was wound into a tight bun, pierced with a hairpin from which a white flower tassel hung. Evidently she liked the color white.

"Well, raising a child is one new experience after another, isn't it. You can never really know what it's like until you've been through it. So much turns out to be different than how you imagined."

"Yes, yes, that's right." I nodded emphatically several times. Here was somebody who seemed to understand. I felt a trust that made me want to reveal my innermost thoughts to her. "It's the difference between thinking that Winnie-the-Pooh is cute, and actually living with a bear."

"Wahahahaha!"

Her burst of raucous laughter took me by surprise. I wouldn't have thought it would be so loud. Nor had I meant to be funny. I was relieved, though, that it was apparently acceptable to say such things. The complaints rolled off my tongue.

"I've been in limbo ever since I had a baby, frustrated at not being able to do the things I want to, and thinking that this isn't how it was supposed to be. Of course I love my daughter, truly, but raising a child is far more difficult than I imagined."

Ms. Komachi stopped laughing. "Children don't just come into the world, do they?" she said. "Giving birth was a huge event in your life, wasn't it?"

"Yes. It gave me great respect for all the mothers of the world."

"Yes, that's right." She gave the faintest of nods, then looked straight into my eyes. "But this is how I see it.

While I do believe that it was hard work for my mother to give birth to me, it also took me every ounce of my own strength to endure the extremely difficult process of being born. After all that time inside my mother's belly growing into a human being with nobody to guide me, all of a sudden I was thrust into an entirely new and strange environment. Imagine what an awful shock it must have been to come in contact with air for the first time, not knowing where I was. Of course I've forgotten what that felt like now. But it's why, whenever I feel happy or glad about something, I count my blessings and think to myself, 'Now, wasn't that worth all the effort of being born?'"

The truth in these words struck me to the core. I was incapable of saying anything in reply.

Ms. Komachi turned toward her computer. "You were the same. Being born is probably the most difficult thing we ever have to do. I am convinced that everything else that comes afterward is nowhere near as hard. If you can survive the ordeal of being born, you can get through anything."

Sitting up ramrod straight, she placed both hands on the keyboard and proceeded to pound the keys with extraordinary speed and dexterity. *Papapapapapapapapa-papapa*—her fingers moved like a machine. I watched, mesmerized, until she finished up with one last light staccato *pa!* Next moment the printer sprang into action with a clatter and ejected a piece of paper that she handed to me. It was a table with a list of book titles with the authors' names and the shelf numbers. I read it through carefully. The first three titles were obviously children's books: *Popon*, *Welcome Back, Piggy Wig* and *Nanno Nonna*. The next, however, was unexpected: *Door to the Moon* by Yukari Ishii.

I knew the name Yukari Ishii because some of my former colleagues in *Mila* followed her online. She posts daily horoscopes on social media. I don't read horoscopes myself, though I know that many young women do. In the past I had actually given some thought to doing a feature on astrology, even if personally I never paid much attention to the monthly horoscope page in *Mila*.

Perhaps Yukari Ishii also wrote picture books? But then I noticed that the book's classification and shelf number were different to those of the other titles.

"Is this about astrology?" I asked.

Ms. Komachi gave no reply. Instead, she bent over to open the third drawer below the counter.

"Please, this is for you."

It was a round, felted woolen object. A blue globe with a mottled green and yellow pattern. The Earth?

"How sweet. Did you make this? My daughter will love it."

"That's a bonus gift for you."

"Pardon?"

"A free gift to go with the book. *Door to the Moon*."

I didn't quite understand. The bewilderment must have shown on my face.

Taking her needle out of the Honeydome box, Ms. Komachi continued: "The good thing about felting is that you can start again halfway through. Even after your project begins to take shape, you can easily change direction along the way if you feel that you want to make something different after all."

"Oh, I see. So it's possible to make something other than what you originally set out to do. That's nice."

Ms. Komachi said nothing. She looked down at the ball of wool once again and began stabbing at it impassively. Apparently she was no longer interested in talking to me.

It was hard to say anything more, with her body language signaling that she had done her duty. I put the globe in the inner pocket of my bag and headed back to the Kids' Space.

Nozomi was reading aloud to Futaba, so I availed myself of the opportunity to go and search for *Door to the Moon*.

It had a striking cover. An intense blue on the front and back, illustrated with a hazy white half-moon. The blue extended even to the page edges—a deep faraway blue that was neither too somber nor too bright. When I opened it, I found inky black on the inside endpapers, and cream-colored pages of text that seemed to float in the surrounding blue. I ran my eyes across the text and started to slip into the same mood I did when reading late at night. Flicking through further, the word "mothers" leaped out at me. My hands stopped.

In the world of astrology the moon signifies mothers, wives, incidents from childhood, emotions, the flesh, changes, and so on.

The moon signifies mothers and wives? That wasn't what I had been led to believe. What about the old adage that a mother is the sun in a family, and the reason why a mother is always supposed to be cheerful and smiling?

My curiosity piqued, I traced back to earlier in the section, where I found something profoundly interesting. Apparently the overlapping of the image of the swollen belly of a pregnant woman's body with the moon is due to the fact that the menstrual cycle and the lunar cycle are in sync. This was followed by observations about its being symbolic both of virginity and of motherhood, with the virgin moon goddess Artemis and the Virgin Mary being given as examples.

Interesting. I liked the author's style. The writing was lovely—easy to read and understand. I was heartened, also, by the fact that this book was about the moon rather than astrology. That gave me more of an affinity with it. What sold me, however, was Yukari Ishii's profile describing her not as an astrologist, but a writer. Curious to know more, I decided to borrow it so I could read it at my leisure.

Returning to the Kids' Space, I located the three books Ms. Komachi had recommended, as well as *Barefoot Gerob*, the one Futaba would not be parted from. Nozomi made me a borrower's card and I took all five books out on loan.

"Fu-*chan* carry!" Sockless inside her shoes, Futaba clutched at *Barefoot Gerob*.

Thank you, thank you, thank you, centipedes and cockroaches, for coming to my rescue this weekend. My gratitude to this author was immense.

～

Another thing I never knew about children until I had one myself is that it is simply impossible to read your own book with a small child in the vicinity. It was Monday morning before I could get past the first few pages of *Door to the Moon*, on the train going to work. In my

Mila days, I used to have no reservations about reading at my desk, since anything could be a potential source of ideas. But in Information Resources I hesitated to do any general reading. Just in case my colleagues might think I was slacking off.

I had just sat down to sort through the mountain of paperwork on my desk when I heard my name called from the doorway. Looking up with a start, I saw Kizawa standing there. I didn't know her well because she had transferred from another company to join the *Mila* team just before I went on maternity leave. She brought with her a reputation as a high-flyer from her previous position working on another publication, and rumor had it that she had been headhunted by our company president. I knew she was single, and about the same age as me, but that was all. The fact I didn't know her well might have been a contributing factor, but she cultivated an overly blasé attitude that really got under my skin. Not to mention that she had taken over from me as the contact for Madam Mizue—another reason I preferred to steer clear of her. To cap it all, while I was on maternity leave, Kizawa was appointed deputy editor in chief.

She thrust a sheet of paper at me. "Can you get this for me?"

I took the document from her. It was a request form for a catalog of a quality brand of bags. She'd obviously come to the door and called to get my attention because she thought my middle-aged male coworkers wouldn't relate to this. Or was she purposely trying to shove her work at *Mila* in my face?

"Will you be able to get hold of it this week?" she asked coolly.

I noticed the bags under her eyes. She wore a loose-knit top and jeans, and the straggly ends of her untidy hair were held back with a barrette. Her outfit told me that she was preparing to stay up all night if necessary. Today was the monthly proofreading deadline for *Mila*. A dark misery slowly welled up inside me. I used to be in her shoes once.

"Yes, I think I can do that," I replied with a determined bright smile to cover my hostility. "Is today proofreading?" I added.

Kizawa patted her hair. "Mmm, yeah."

"Lucky you. Being an editor is so rewarding."

This was intended as light small talk. Kizawa's response, however, was to look away for a moment. Then with an awkward smile she said, "But it feels like I'm always at work and never at home. Sometimes I don't even make the last train and have to cough up for a taxi at my own expense. Just once, I'd like to leave the office on time, too."

Too? A dull pain burned in my chest.

"And even when I do get home early, there's nobody there. It's lonely," she continued.

What could I say to that? Nothing. I merely tried to smile diplomatically. Was it my imagination, or was I right in thinking that Kizawa sounded completely jealous, of *me*? The idea of her haggard and worn out, choking on her jealousy of me, was a thought I found disturbing.

Why don't you quit if you want to go home so badly! I wanted to yell at her. *You chose to accept the job, you're in it because you want to be.*

But I knew it cut both ways. I had made my own choices too. I chose to have a child. But am I not supposed to want both? Is it too much to want to have a child *and* a satisfying career? Am *I* not allowed to voice my dissatisfaction?

I stood there, mute, until Kizawa broke the silence. "Oh, and another thing. Ms. Kanata is giving a talk the day after tomorrow."

Instantly I perked up. Madam Mizue?

"We aren't the sponsor, so there's no obligation, but the editor in chief is making noises about someone putting in an appearance. My hands are full, though, so I wondered if you could go, Ms. Sakitani?"

"Yes!"

Kizawa's shoulder gave a startled twitch at my reaction.

"Okay, I'll send details by email. Thanks. I'll get the chief to contact the head of Information Resources and square it with him too."

This last was said with her back already turned as she walked off down the corridor. I didn't care what she thought of me—I was simply glad she had asked. I was going to see Madame Mizue. *Yes!* As her former editor. At last, I had something to do that was work befitting an editor.

~

During my lunch break the next day, I went to a bookshop and bought Madam Mizue's latest novel. Today was its launch, the reason for the talk, I assumed—PR for her latest book.

The event was to be held the next day in a city hotel from 11 a.m. I emailed Madam Mizue to say I would attend and received a reply inviting me to have tea afterward.

My cup runneth over! I was so thrilled.

On the train going to collect Futaba, I tried to race through the new book but did not get even halfway through. Tonight I would simply have to get Futaba to sleep early.

The whole way home from daycare, Futaba was singing a song she had learned that day. She was so obsessed with it that even after we got home, she hummed it end-lessly to the accompaniment of her own dancing. After her bath I tucked her into her futon, lay down beside her, then turned the bedroom light low and patted her rhythmically on the chest to lull her to sleep.

"Off to bye-byes now."

But she would not fall asleep. Instead, wide-awake, she raised her voice mischievously loud and started to sing again.

"That's enough, close your eyes!" I chided her.

This only had the opposite effect. "No! Fu-*chan* sing song!" Even more excited now, she jumped up and planted her legs on the futon with arms akimbo.

Oh, where was Shuji? If only I knew when he would be home, it would be a whole lot less stressful just to know that help was on the way. But I hadn't heard a thing from him.

Eventually giving up, I turned on the lights and lay down next to Futaba, then opened up Madam Mizue's book. Futaba continued to sing before opening the pic-ture book next to her pillow. No doubt in imitation of me. She looked at the pictures while chatting away. I suspected she wanted me to read to her, but I ignored her and continued to read my own book. Every minute was precious.

149

Madam Mizue's novel was everything I expected. I could imagine the discussions she and her editor would have had, and in my head tried to dissect their approach to the story. Ah, if only I could do that too. But it was hopeless.

At some point I lost concentration and in spite of myself I dropped off to sleep. I didn't even notice Shuji arrive home. And my book was still not finished.

~

The next morning Futaba awoke sneezing and with a runny nose. I put my hand to her forehead apprehensively. Not too hot. With a prayer in my heart, I held her in my arms and stuck the thermometer under her arm.

"Is Futaba all right?" Shuji asked casually. It was my fault I'd fallen asleep with the air conditioner on, but I was angry with him for not setting the off-switch timer when he went to bed.

The thermometer beeped. Her temperature was 36.9 degrees. A little on the high side, but not too much cause for concern. *Please, let her be all right—today of all days.*

Hesitantly I asked Shuji, "Um, I don't suppose…"

"What?"

"I'm sure there'll be no problem, but just in case…just

in case there's a call from daycare today, I don't suppose you could pick her up?"

"Ah, no, can't do that. I have to go over to Maku-hari today."

"I was just checking."

I got Futaba ready and took her to daycare. On the train I continued speed-reading Madam Mizue's book. I couldn't very well not know how it ended. Somehow I managed to scan through it entirely and reach the end.

But this was not how I wanted to read anything written by Madam Mizue. I would have far preferred to be reading her in a quiet place, sitting down and relaxed. Yet it couldn't be helped.

Thanks to Kizawa alerting my boss, I was able to excuse myself at 10 a.m. and went to the bathroom to freshen up. Just as I was leaving, my smartphone rang.

"Tsukushi Daycare" appeared on the screen.

Ignore it. Pretend you didn't notice.

Now is the time to step up as a parent!

Two voices wrestled in my mind.

The phone stopped ringing and switched to voicemail. I waited for the recorded message to finish before pressing the button and putting the phone to my ear. Mayu, Futaba's class teacher, had left a message to say Futaba had a fever and to please come and collect her.

151

What if... What if I pretend I didn't hear this?

Daycare would contact my office and someone there would try and phone me. Perhaps I could just ignore the call, and say I left my smartphone at home. That would be one option.

Or, I could give up on the idea of tea with Madam Mizue, and contact daycare as soon as the talk finished to say I would hurry and be there by 2 p.m. That much at least would be forgivable, wouldn't it? It wasn't as if Futaba wasn't in a safe place at daycare.

An image of Futaba's tearful face came into my mind. Maybe she had wormed out from under her duvet last night and had been chilled by the air conditioner. Now she could be suffering from a high fever that was all my fault because I did not get her to sleep early and fell asleep myself instead. A wave of guilt washed over me at the memory of her opening up the picture book while I ignored her. I was a terrible mother.

If I didn't go to the talk, it would no doubt confirm the opinion Kizawa and the *Mila* deputy editor in chief had of me as unreliable. But if I didn't go, it wouldn't be a disaster. It's just that I wanted to go.

I screwed my eyes shut tight. Taking a deep breath, I rang daycare back.

~

On my way, I phoned Kizawa to tell her I couldn't go to the talk. "That's fine. Take care," was all she said. I do not understand that woman at all.

When I arrived, Futaba pattered over with a big smile on her face. She looked perfectly all right to me.

"Look at you! I thought you had a temperature of 37.8 and no energy."

Mayu came over. She had just turned twenty-eight and had only recently been appointed as a class teacher.

"She looked peaky earlier, but was only a bit sleepy after all, it seems. Her temperature is down to 37.1 now."

That was a relief, but I felt despondent that I needn't have come after all. When today was such a special day. Before I knew it, I was crying.

"Oh dear, you must have been worried," Mayu said, with an understanding smile.

In a low, strangled voice that I didn't even recognize as mine, I turned to her and said, "Why is it always the women?"

Mayu looked shocked. She probably had no idea what I meant. But almost always, it is women who pick up children from daycare. Why is the parent who gives birth *always* expected to make the biggest career sacrifice?

"Um, if the children have a temperature over 37.5, we

are supposed to contact the parent…we don't want them to have a fit or anything," she said nervously.

I came to my senses. Mayu must have thought I was blaming her.

"It's not that. I'm sorry. Thank you very much."

Holding Futaba in my arms, I punched the time card and left the daycare center.

∼

Once we were back home, I measured Futaba's temperature again and found it had gone down even more, to 36.5.

That evening I gave her some of her favorite apple yogurt for dessert, and afterward she happily lined up her stuffed toys on the table to play with. Hopeful of getting her to bed early, I put her pyjamas on at eight.

"Time for bed now."

"No."

"You don't want to get another fever, do you? Look, Bunny is tidying up."

"No tidy up."

No, no, no.

"Mummy doesn't want to tidy up either."

Sighing, I picked up Futaba and her stuffed rabbit to carry them off to bed. We lay curled up together on the futon while Futaba prattled away to the rabbit.

~

I had sent Madam Mizue an apology from the train. "Don't mind. These things happen. You never know what will happen next with children. We'll meet another time," came her reply almost immediately.

You never know what will happen next with children. Like a child getting a fever on a special day for the mother… Madam Mizue had raised two sons herself, so she must have had similar experiences. Oh, I did so want to talk to her! But I wasn't an editor anymore. I was in no position to casually suggest we meet for a cup of tea.

Come to think of it, that was one of the things I liked most about being an editor. The opportunity to see the people I wanted to see, to sit down with them one-on-one and have in-depth conversations.

Why did I feel so exhausted? When I was at *Mila* I was never like this. It didn't matter how busy I was, or how much rushing around I had to do, I was always fine. Now my body felt stiff and cumbersome, like clay, and so did my spirit.

As I lay there with these thoughts churning in my head, the tears began pouring out again. Before I knew it I was fast asleep.

~

When I opened my eyes it was 11.30. Yet again, I had fallen asleep while trying to get Futaba down early and was left with not enough time to do all the things I had planned. It was depressing.

Futaba was sleeping peacefully. I placed my hand on her forehead to check. Her skin was far from feverish, cold if anything. I stroked her hair a little and then stood up. Shuji had still not arrived home. The apartment was untidy; unwashed dishes were piled in the sink and washing I'd brought in earlier lay tossed on the sofa, still on the hangers it had dried on. With a sigh, I set about tidying, starting with the laundry.

I heard the sound of the key in the lock. Shuji.

"I'm home."

"You're late."

"Uh, yeah, I was busy," he said, brushing quickly past me. But he didn't look tired from work to me. I caught a whiff of alcohol.

"Have you been drinking?"

"Huh? Uh–huh. Just a bit."

"So you won't need dinner, then?"

Shuji winced at the irritation in my voice. "I got caught up for just one drink, that's all. Sometimes you feel like doing that, don't you?"

"Yes, I do. I most certainly do. But I can't, can I."

Once I'd started, I couldn't stop. The floodgate burst, releasing a deluge of angry words. "Why am I always the one who takes Futaba to daycare and picks her up, and has to make dinner, not knowing if you're going to be there to eat it or not? I had somewhere I wanted to go today, too, but I was called in by daycare, wasn't I, even though it turned out to be nothing. I always have to hurry because I never have enough time, but I put myself last all the time, and even though there are a million things I'd like to do, I can't!"

"Hey, it's not like I went out for a night on the town!"

"But you went out drinking, without even telling me!"

I threw the towel I'd just finished folding up at him. The only reason I didn't throw a mug was because I would have to clean up the mess if it broke. Even in moments like this, with the blood rushing to my head, I was making those split-second kind of calculations.

"She's your child too. When I was pregnant, didn't you say we'd do all the work together? Well, how about helping me more with housework and daycare!"

"Don't you care about my promotion prospects? Do you want me to not get promoted? You know I can't skip meetings or business trips to pick up Futaba, or come home early enough to cook dinner. The reality is you're the one with a job flexible enough for you to leave at five o'clock."

I held my tongue. There was a part of me that did think it would not suit me for Shuji's position and potential for promotion to be compromised. But it didn't feel fair. I'd stepped off *my* career track, hadn't I? Why did I have to be the one who shouldered all responsibilities at home? Because I was the mother?

"But I'm the only one who loses out," I spit out tearfully.

I saw the distaste come over his face and his mouth open to speak, then suddenly stop as his eyes widened in surprise. Futaba was standing at the door to the living room. Our bickering had woken her.

"Fu-*chan* tidy up," she said in a quavering voice. Then she began picking up her stuffed toys to carry them over to the toy box. The sight of her face on the verge of tears tore at my heart. She may not have understood our words exactly, but she knew that we were arguing because of her. Maybe she was thinking that by being a good girl, we would stop. I grabbed her from behind in a big hug.

I'm sorry, Futaba, my precious daughter, so sorry! What was I thinking, talking about losing out?

She is the child I had longed for. How could I even think of blaming her for my life not going to plan?

~

The next day I received a phone call at work on the
internal line. It was Madam Mizue, calling me from reception. I knew immediately why she'd done this. Phoning me on the company line rather than my smartphone
would make it easier for me to leave my desk. Going
down to the lobby, I found her wearing a kimono and
beaming genially at me.

Oh, how I had wanted to see her so much! But at the
unexpected sight of her, all of a sudden I came undone,
and tears rolled down my face.

She was unruffled. Placing one hand gently on my
shoulder, she murmured, "When does your break start?
We can have lunch together, if you'd like."

With a smile she mentioned the name of an informal
bistro near the office and told me she would wait there.

~

Madam Mizue was visiting the Banyusha office for
a meeting with Kizawa. Apparently *The Pink Plane Tree*
was going to be made into a film. I was bitter at the
thought of Kizawa handling the project, the novel I
had worked so hard on with Madam Mizue to bring
to fruition.

As she raised a spoonful of omelet rice to her mouth, Madam Mizue said, "Did you realize, Ms. Sakitani, that it was a teeny bit stressful for me writing the instalments for the novel?"

"It was?"

"Oh my, yes. Think how nerve-racking it is to write for all those sensitive, impressionable young women. I was always worrying about being inadvertently insensitive, or laughed at for being out of touch and too old-fashioned." Swallowing a mouthful of omelet, she went on cheerfully: "Yes, it was a teeny bit stressful, but so much fun—tremendous fun, in fact. In the course of writing it, I realized that there is so much I have to tell young women. And the whole time those two main characters were constantly chatting away in my head. We were always together. They were like daughters to me, as were my readers—all my precious daughters. It was like having children again, after a very long time."

Mizue crinkled her eyes up in a smile.

"It was all thanks to you, Ms. Sakitani. You were there for the birth of my book and we raised it together. You were midwife, nurse, mother and father, for me and for the novel."

At this, the tears poured down. "I was afraid I would never be able to see you again," I said, covering my face in both hands. "Because I'm not an…"

I'm not an editor. The surge of emotion that I had so far managed to keep in check broke through the dam. "I'm so jealous of Kizawa working on *Mila*, and I can't help thinking that my life is out of control because of my daughter, but I hate myself for even thinking it."

Madam Mizue put down her spoon. "Ah, Ms. Sakitani, so you're on the merry-go-round, too," she said gently.

"The merry-go-round?"

With a chuckle she smiled at me. "It's a very common condition," she said with apparent relish. "Singles are envious of those who are married, and married couples envy those with children, but people with children are envious of singles. It's an endless merry-go-round. But isn't that funny? That each person should be chasing the tail of the person in front of them, when no one is coming first or last. In other words, when it comes to happiness nothing is better or worse—there is no definitive state."

Madam Mizue took a sip of water.

"Life is one revelation after another. Things don't always go to plan, no matter what your circumstances. But the flip side is all the unexpected, wonderful things that you could never have imagined happening. Ultimately it's all for the best that many things don't turn out the way we hoped. Try not to think of upset plans or schedules as personal failure or bad luck. If you can do that, then you can change, in your own self and in your life overall."

Then she looked off into the distance and smiled.

～

After the meal I stretched out my hand at the till to wrestle the bill from Madam Mizue. Though I could not put the lunch down as a company expense, it was nevertheless imprinted in my brain that I should pay.

Madam Mizue held the bill up high. "No, please let this be my treat."

"But…"

"For your birthday. It's coming up soon, isn't it? That's why the *natsu* character for summer is in your name, isn't it? Natsumi."

I might have mentioned that to her at one time. She had remembered.

"Thank you very much, then. I appreciate it." I bowed my head in thanks.

"So how old will you be?" Madam Mizue asked mischievously.

"Forty."

"Ah, how nice. Finally you're ready to do all kinds of things. Have fun, the playground is big." She took my hands and squeezed them tight. "Happy birthday, Natsumi. I'm so glad I met you."

A feeling of tranquillity began to flow through me, seeping into every cell of my body. My time at *Mila* had given me not only a career, but this too. In a place away from the office, it had gifted me with the warmth of emotion I felt in this moment. *This* was worth being born for, I thought, from the bottom of my heart.

~

That night, Futaba went straight to sleep, unusually for her. Shuji was still not home, so I covered up his dinner and settled myself on the sofa with *Door to the Moon*. Before long I reached a chapter with the rather striking title of "The Two Eyes of the Heart." I brought my face closer to the page and read on.

The heart has two eyes to perceive that which is not visible to the eye. One is the "Sun Eye," which sheds a bright light on our understanding of things from a rational and logical perspective. The other is the "Moon Eye," which perceives things through instinct or emotion, in our imagination or dreams, such as seeing ghosts in the dark or entertaining a secret love. Both eyes exist in our hearts.

For the first time in a very long while, I also felt capable of immersing myself in a book with a clear head. I continued to read, becoming deeply engrossed by what lay under the beautiful blue cover. I found the connections between the sun and moon in mythology to be fascinating, as were explanations of how to interpret astrology and magic, and the hidden emotions of human beings.

From big things to little, there are some things we simply cannot force to go to plan, no matter how hard we try.

It was a surprise to see the words "go to plan." The same words Madam Mizue had said to me earlier in the day. How uncanny the way what one reads can sometimes synchronize with reality.

My estimation of Ms. Komachi went up. I wonder why she told me about this book.

Which reminded me…the free gift she gave me was still in my bag. I dug the felted object out from the inside pocket and sat it lightly on my palm to examine. The continents on the Ping-Pong-ball-sized globe were mostly rough outlines, but Japan was accurately rendered. Perhaps the fine, detailed handiwork that had gone into making it was a sign of love of the country. A way of saying, *This is where I am.* It's night now. The Earth will turn and morning will come...

While rolling the felted globe in my fingers, I was struck by an idea: Ptolemaic theory and Copernican theory; geocentrism and heliocentrism. Eons ago, people used to believe that the Earth was stationary and the heavens moved around it. When in fact it was the Earth that rotated.

Something clicked. *That's it.*

I was *forced* to move from *Mila* to the information resources department. And I *have* to do housework and childcare. If I put myself at the center of everything, does that mean I always see myself as a victim? And why I always end up wondering why can't people do things that work for me.

I stared at the blue sphere on my palm. The Earth moves. Morning and night don't *stay*—they *go*.

What do I want to do now? Where do I want to go?

I was aware of something shifting. The same gut feeling I had had that morning with Madam Mizue moved more sharply into focus. Suddenly, I knew what I wanted: I wanted to be a literary-fiction editor and work with authors, to draw out the best in them and bring readers the best possible stories.

The playground is big. Madam Mizue's words still rang in my head. Had she been suggesting I get off the merry-go-round and try out something else in the playground? Never swerving from a path is not necessarily a virtue— isn't it better sometimes to be honest about what you really want?

I picked up my smartphone to search for recruiting information with publishers. Up until now, I had limited myself to companies that published magazines, thinking that was my only option. But my current situation meant that being part of a magazine editorial team, which requires speed and teamwork, was not feasible. In book publishing, however, it might be easier to work independently at my own pace. Maybe I could find a new path? Would it be possible for me to change direction and go into literary publishing?

After a while I came across Cherry Peach Books, an old established publishing company that is strong in literary fiction. Madam Mizue had also published several books with them. As luck would have it, they were currently recruiting, but I would have to post my application by tomorrow. I might just be in time.

I tried to keep my rising excitement in check as I pored over what was required. After today's meeting with Madam Mizue, and Futaba going to sleep early, I felt as if perhaps the tide was changing. As if there were greater forces on my side now.

~

The next day, Saturday, I paid another visit to the Community House library. By myself this time, while Shuji stayed at home with Futaba. Today was the due date for the library books, which I returned to Nozomi at the counter. She noticed me glance in the direction of the reference corner.

"Miss Himeno is on her break now. She'll back very soon."

"Miss Himeno?"

"Oh!" Nozomi's hand flew to her mouth.

"Ms. Komachi used to be my teacher at elementary school. She was the school nurse and teacher for children with special educational needs. Sometimes I forget to use her married name."

Oh, so Ms. Komachi used to work in a school? She had been a school nurse and special-needs teacher.

Next moment, Ms. Komachi herself arrived back. Her large body swayed as she walked by, looking at me impassively. I waited until she was settled behind her counter before going over.

"Thank you for your help the other day. I loved *Door to the Moon*."

"Uh-huh," she answered laconically, without changing expression.

167

"But I read it too quickly, skating over parts of it, so I'm going to buy it. I think it's a book I want to own."

Ms. Komachi shifted and leaned back slightly in her seat. "I'm happy to hear that. It's nice to know I was able to connect you with a book you not only wanted to read, but want to have with you always."

"Yes. I want to try and change. Thanks to this book."

A broad smile lit Ms. Komachi's face. "You may say that it was the book, but it's how you read a book that is most valuable, rather than any power it might have itself."

I liked this idea. Pleased at her response and emboldened at being spoken to so warmly, I leaned forward. "Ms. Komachi, I heard you used to be a special-needs teacher. Does that mean you changed career?"

"Uh-huh. I started out as librarian in a big library. Then I went back to study and became a special-needs teacher. Then I became a librarian again."

"Why did you change career once and then go back?"

I heard a crack from her neck as she swiveled her head.

"It's just how things worked out. I went with the flow and did what was easiest at the time to achieve what I wanted. Moment by moment—circumstances always change, quite independently from what we want to do. A family situation, for example, or health issues, or a job might go when a company folds, or one could fall in love out of the blue."

"Fall in love?" I repeated, without thinking.

She touched the floral hairpin in her bun. "This was the most unexpected thing that ever happened to me. Never did I imagine someone like the person who gave me this appearing in my life."

Did she mean her husband? My curiosity was piqued and I would have liked to probe further, but it was not a topic one could ask too much about.

"Are you glad you changed careers? Didn't you feel anxious about it?"

"Things change, even if you want them to stay the same. At the same time, you can try to change, but you will still remain the same."

She dragged the Honeydome box to the edge of the counter. Seeing her pull out the felting needle, I understood. My time was over. Sure enough, Ms. Komachi's face became blank as she began pricking with her needle again.

~

After I returned home, Shuji got the car out and all three of us went shopping at Eden, a general merchandise store that sells everything from food to household

169

necessities. I wanted to stock up on rice, drinks and other bulky items, as well as buy Futaba some new underwear and T-shirts.

"Do you mind if I drop by ZAZ?" I asked Shuji, and he took Futaba off to the children's play area to wait for me. Everything is so much easier when he's around at weekends.

ZAZ is a chain of eyeglasses shops. I generally don't have much of a problem with my eyes in everyday life, but I do use disposable contact lenses on occasion. I had not bought any for six months and my stock was running low.

"Excuse me," I called to the assistant's back. When he turned around, I was amazed to find I knew him. "Kiriyama!"

Kiriyama had been employed by an editorial production company I used to commission work from when I was at *Mila*.

"Ms. Sakitani? Oh! What a surprise to see you here."

"What are you doing here?"

"I quit the production company and started here last month."

It was actually a relief to see him there, looking healthy and smiling. He used to be so thin I worried about him sometimes, but now he had filled out and his color was better. To tell the truth, I had always thought that the

way that company operated was ridiculous. They would
take on any kind of job: a ten-page spread on street pho-
tography, for example, or researching thirty ramen restaurants in one day. Since they did anything we asked,
it made things easy for us, but I could well imagine the
superhuman effort staff would have to make to fulfil
such commissions.

"You're looking well, Ms. Sakitani. You had a baby,
didn't you?"

"Yes. Actually I'm thinking of changing jobs, too," I
let slip, feeling a bond with him as a former work colleague. "I'd like to work in book publishing rather than
magazines. I applied to Cherry Peach and am waiting to
hear back. So I'm a bit on tenterhooks at the moment. I
should know soon."

"You brought out that book by Mizue Kanata, didn't
you? It was a big hit. *The Pink Plane Tree* was appealing
even to a guy, like me."

I was heartened to hear this. Kiriyama took my member's card with him and disappeared out the back.

"Excuse me, but are you in a hurry for these?" he asked
when he returned, looking rather apologetic. "We're out
of this brand of lens at the moment. I can order more
in straight away and let you know when they arrive,"
he continued in a smooth, practiced tone. For someone

who had only started last month, he was a natural. The work suited him.

"I hope it goes well with Cherry Peach," Kiriyama said as I left. "Even just knowing what you want to do is a great thing."

I'd always thought well of Kiriyama, and my opinion was confirmed after seeing him again in the eyeglasses shop. He came over as smart, confident and pleasant, and left a good impression.

Things change. I change, other people change. That's a good thing. My heart was already at Cherry Peach. Oh, the wonderful books I would produce once I was there…

～

What I received, however, was a dry email of rejection. I was very upset, as I had been confident of making it through the first round of screening at least. I had assumed that the fact this publisher had released some of Madam Mizue's books would be to my advantage. But I had failed to get even an interview.

I knew there was no hope for me. It was futile to try and change jobs at my age, with a small child. My only experience with book publishing had been that one title, which may have sold well, but if that seemed like a one-off fluke to anyone, I'm not sure that I could blame them. Applicants looking for a mid-career change need to have a range of skills to be immediately useful, in order to have an edge in the job market. A major publishing house such as Cherry Peach would no doubt attract a pool of talent with far more experience than I had. I should have realized that, had I given it more thought.

To add to my woes, Kizawa was promoted to editor in chief of *Mila*, a further blow to my ego. When it was announced at the morning meeting, she responded in her usual manner with a brusque comment and defiant thrust of her chin.

But then, in the wave of congratulatory applause, I caught something. It was a glimpse of a blush, the ghost of a smile on her lips and a damp glitter at the edges of her eyelids that gave her away. Instantly my jealousy evaporated. Kizawa, too, had struggled and fought her own battles, too, to get where she was. She wasn't taking this promotion for granted, and was in fact deeply moved. I have no doubt it had been a tough road for her. I should have been more understanding, and regretted saying "Lucky you" to her in such an offhand way.

The merry-go-round had stopped. I was someone else now, on a different path. I had mine and she had hers. We each would travel through our own landscape.

Kizawa caught sight of me clapping vigorously, and the corners of her mouth turned up, just a fraction.

~

Two days later it was my birthday. Shuji had arranged to come home early and all three of us went out for dinner. Over our meal, I told him about my application to Cherry Peach and my dismal failure. He could not believe it. In fact, he was so astonished to hear I wanted to quit Banyusha after so many years, as well as how difficult it was to find a new job, that I realized he had not really understood how I had been feeling. However, it also occurred to me that I might not have actually explained my feelings to him before. All this time I'd been grumbling and complaining without making it clear why. It was my turn to be astonished when Shuji turned out to be unexpectedly sympathetic.

We decided that from the following week Shuji would take charge of Futaba's morning daycare drop-off. Since picking her up was more difficult for him, I would do it, but he would learn the ropes for the morning run. He listened intently, taking notes as I explained everything, including how to change the futon cover on Monday morning.

"When you get emotional and say things like 'help me' or 'do more,' I don't really know what to do. But if you explain it logically and give me specific suggestions, I can understand."

I saw his point. I needed to use the "Sun Eye" more, to keep it in balance with the "Moon Eye."

Despite my complaints, I know that Shuji, in his own way, is thinking of his family. And we have Futaba between the two of us, growing more expressive by the day. Hearing her say "Happee" in a faltering little voice was unbearably adorable.

The three of us create our family together, one day at a time. And I do so much want to make the most of this time. "Go with the flow," To borrow Ms. Komachi's words. Perhaps my failure with Cherry Peach was a sign that being an editor was not ideal for now. Yet my heart demurred in protest, and I hid my feelings by gulping down the rest of my tea.

I had just sat down again after getting a refill of herb tea from the bar when my smartphone rang with a number I didn't recognize. Signaling to Shuji, I stood up to take the call outside.

"This is Kiriyama from ZAZ."

"Oh hi." I immediately relaxed at the sound of his friendly voice. The summer night breeze outside was pleasant.

"Your contact lenses have arrived. Sorry to keep you waiting."

"Thank you. I'll drop by to collect them."

"Um, but that was actually an excuse to call you."

"Sorry?" It was noisy in the background on the other end of the line. Kiriyama didn't sound as if he was calling from the shop, where he would have used a landline, not a mobile phone.

I heard him take a deep breath at the other end before saying, "Ms. Sakitani, have you heard back from Cherry Peach yet?"

"Yes. I didn't get the position."

"Oh, that's good," he replied automatically, then apologized with an awkward laugh. "I'm sorry," he said. "It's just that one of my university acquaintances works in the editorial department at Maple Publications."

Maple Publications? I knew it as a reputable publisher of picture books and children's literature. *Barefoot Gerob* was one of theirs.

"She's resigning next month because her husband has been transferred overseas and she's going too, so her position will be advertised. But she said if they find a good candidate before then, well, you know. So I thought of you."

My heart beat faster and I was unable to speak as Kiriyama's voice streamed from the smartphone gripped tightly in my hand.

"I think you and Maple Publications would be a good fit. An old established publisher like Cherry Peach with a pure literature department is fine, but Maple has a good vibe and seems to have a flexible company culture. They're always doing something new. If you want, I can speak with my friend and arrange for you to meet the head of the editorial department."

"But I'm forty, and I have a two-year-old child."

"Yeah, I thought of that. But having a child would be a plus at a place like Maple, seeing as how they specialize in children's books. My friend is also a working mother."

The wave of hope in my heart continued to surge, even as all the reasons that would count against me lined up in my head.

"But I have no experience of editing children's books. None whatsoever."

"Literary editing and children's books are separate departments. Maple also puts out lots of great books for adults too."

Though no title immediately sprang to mind, I conceded he might be right about that. In that case, then... well, maybe I could do something in the general literary section.

"Ms. Sakitani, you didn't just concentrate on fashion at *Mila*, did you? You put together features on all sorts of topics that appeal to young women. And that page 'Let's Try Again Tomorrow'—that always gave me a boost when I read it. I'm sure that's why you were able to bring out a novel like *The Pink Plane Tree*. When you said you wanted to switch to literary editing, I was really pleased."

My heart sang. To think that somebody at close quarters had seen and recognized what I'd done.

"Kiriyama, why are you doing this for me?"

I simply wanted to know. I wasn't a friend of his, nor did he have any kind of obligation to me—he was just someone I used to know at work.

He answered without hesitation. "There is no 'why.' It's just the way things turned out. Isn't it a good thing to want more great books in the world? I want to read them too."

I looked down at the ground. My feet shook in their sandals.

Kiriyama said he would be in touch and we hung up. I was walking on air as I made my way back to the table, where I drank down my herb tea in one gulp.

"What's up?" Shuji asked.

I told him what had happened.

"That sounds like a fantastic opportunity!" he said. He clearly understood. But I was quailing inside. It was too good. Besides, I was just getting over my disappointment about Cherry Peach, and if I let my hopes rise only to be dashed again, the hurt would come back.

"Does this kind of thing really happen? It's too good to be true. I can't believe an opportunity like this would just fall into my lap."

Shuji looked at me. "You're wrong," he said earnestly. "This didn't just come to you. It happened because you did something for yourself. You took action and that caused things to change around you."

I stared at him, and he smiled at me reassuringly. "You made this opportunity happen."

Well, maybe I did. I'd missed out with Cherry Peach. But if I hadn't gone for a job with them, there would have been no reason to tell Kiriyama I wanted to be a literary editor. The thing that I had started had ended up making a connection in an unexpected place and borne fruit. Kiriyama's offer may have been a complete surprise, but one I wholeheartedly welcomed.

Shuji patted Futaba lightly on the head as she finished her ice cream. "Fu-*chan*, how about you and I head home together?"

"What?"

"I'm thinking you probably want to go to a bookshop, Natsumi. Am I right? There's one near the station that'd still be open."

Futaba looked at the two of us in alarm.

"Fu-*chan*, how would you feel if Mommy wanted something but she couldn't have it and was crying inside all the time?" Shuji asked.

"Fu-*chan* sad," she said in a small voice.

~

Leaving Futaba and Shuji, I took myself off to the Meishin bookshop inside the train station building. I was in search of anything published by Maple: picture books, nursery tales, children's books and—as Kiriyama had said—any of their numerous bestselling general titles for adults.

It wasn't long before I realized, to my surprise, that I had already read and loved quite a few novels from Maple. Still in a daze, I scrutinized the shelves and selected several other titles that I liked the look of. Then I added *Barefoot Gerob* to my pile of purchases. Lastly, I searched for *Door to the Moon*. But the striking blue cover was nowhere to be found. Instead, I found the same title with a different cover: *Door to the Moon* in a new format. A graceful picture of the moon filled almost the entire front cover, against a background of deep blue graduating to yellowy green at the bottom. When I opened the book, the endpapers were not the inky black of the previous edition, but a startling canary yellow. The text inside appeared to be the same, however.

It was a reissue: proof that this book was beloved and still in demand. The knowledge warmed me. Books, too, could be reborn. I thought of who might pick up this book and how they might react to it.

Ah… I did so want to make books.

Books that made one look forward to tomorrow, or helped reveal hidden depths within oneself.

While I had been engrossed in reading my edition of *Door to the Moon*, I hadn't realized that its beautiful night-sky cover had undergone a makeover, and though the inside was the still the same, now it looked as if moonlight was beaming out from it. Meanwhile, the tiny black-and-white motif of a moon waxing and waning, which had been on the bottom right-hand corner of every even-numbered page in my edition, had been moved to the top in the new one. What was once below had risen higher—changing position but still the same.

I, too, could change, and still be the same inside.

Any parent who tries to give their child the dream of Santa Claus is allowing the truth of him to dwell in their own heart. And this is why children believe confidently in the existence of Santa Claus riding on his sleigh.

I continue my reading in the winter sunlight when the telephone rings.

"Hello, Maple Publications editorial department," I say as I pick up the receiver.

At the meeting Kiriyama had immediately set up with Maple, I was asked two questions by the editor in chief. How did I go about managing the production of the novel with Madam Mizue? And what kind of books did I want to make in future? The editor nodded, listening attentively to my heartfelt response.

Everything I had learned at *Mila*—from the production work on the magazine to what I had begun to think about after being transferred—came to my aid in formulating my vision for the next iteration of my future self. Banyusha had provided me with everything that was essential for reaching this point. There was value in all my experience. This appreciation of my own effort and my gratitude to Banyusha gave me a solid base to stand on.

∽

I ask the person on the other end of the line to please wait a moment, and push the hold button.

"Imae-*san*, call from Ms. Watahashi," I tell my colleague at the desk opposite, and transfer the call through to her. Imae's six-year-old daughter, Miho-*chan*, sits in a fold-up seat next to her, reading the picture book open in front of her while her mother speaks on the phone to an author she is working with.

Miho-*chan*'s classes at school were suddenly cancelled because of a flu outbreak.

Ms. Arakawa, editor in chief of the children's books department, comes over to the desk. When she notices Miho, she leans over and asks gently, "What do you think of this book. Is it interesting?"

The book is the second in a series put out by Maple. It's about tiny people who make burrows in the ground, in lots of different holes.

"Yes, it's funny. I like Buchi the dog with the brown back. He looks like a hamburger," Miho responds brightly.

"A hamburger? Goodness. I never thought of that."

Another passing staff member looks at Miho, one of our precious, treasured readers, and smiles. There is no resistance to children being in this workplace. Here, they are welcome. I was amazed the first time I saw a member of staff away on parental leave come in with a baby. Everybody flocked to see the baby and the company president even held it.

Ms. Arakawa comes over to my desk and hands me some color photocopies of an illustration. "Ms. Sakitani, would you mind asking Futaba-*chan* which one she likes?"

"Yes, I'd be happy to."

"Thank you, as always."

Until now, a child had been an obstacle in my workplace. Here, they are not only accepted, but regarded as useful.

Ms. Arakawa leaves and I turn my attention back to the book.

The Santa Claus that parents teach is not a lie, but part of a larger truth. Likewise, do the eyes of the sun and moon in our hearts cooperate, without denying each other's existence, in formulating our perceptions of the world.

I have read this page in the new-format *Door to the Moon* so many times I can say it by heart. This passage is underlined, in order to inscribe it into my mind.

When I started working at Maple, I had a revelation. I realized that when one reads or writes a novel, it is the Moon Eye that is in play. But when one works on a manuscript to help get it into shape before sending it into the world, the Sun Eye comes to the fore. Both eyes are essential. From now on, I will try to keep both of mine wide open, letting them work together, neither at the expense of the other.

I close the book and carefully put it back with the others between the bookends on my desk. Then I take out a thin pamphlet, a serial novel that I came across last month.

Yes, this is it! I thought at the time. Here is an author I passionately want to work with and cultivate. Drawing on all my networks, I managed to obtain his email address and am now about to try and make contact. I calm my breathing and turn to the computer. Slowly, I tap out an email that come straight from the heart: *I would like to open a new door with you.*

~

The Earth goes around.

We gaze at the moon, illuminated by the sun.

Feet on the ground and facing the sky, we go forward, changing as we do.

In order to deliver a larger truth to the person looking down at an open page.

4

Hiroya, 30, NEET
(not in employment, education or training)

The bunch I hung out with as a kid taught me a lot. They weren't always human, or from Earth, and they came from anywhere in time, ranging from the prehistoric past to the distant future, sometimes even other dimensions. But they were my buddies. More real to me than my classmates ever were. I never got bored when I was with them. They were cool, fun to be with, brave and kind. They fought evil with their special powers and won the heart of the prettiest girl. I always got a thrill at seeing them, no matter how often we met.

So what happened? How come time moved on for me only? Eventually, as I turned thirty, I overtook even the ones who'd always been older than me. Without becoming anything at all.

~

It's Friday afternoon and I'm sitting on the sofa watching TV. Mom dumps her bag of vegetables on the kitchen table.

"They had these great big daikon today—Miura daikon, they're called. February's the season for them. They were enormous!"

She unpacks potatoes, carrots and apples from her flowery eco shopping bag. These are big too.

"I wanted to buy one, but with all this, it was too much to carry home."

She pulls out a Chinese cabbage.

"I'd like to go back to get one, but it's too embarrassing. People would look at me and think *Here she is again*. Besides, I must get ready for work soon."

I say nothing, but I know this is aimed at me.

~

There's a place called a community house near here. Joined to the local elementary school. I was at high school when we moved here, so I've never seen it. But Mom sometimes goes there for flower-arranging classes. They do courses and that kind of thing. Once every three months there's a farmers' market that sells vegetables and fruit direct from producers. That's where Mom went today.

"Hiroya, would you go back for me?"

"Yeah, all right."

I point the remote at the TV and switch off. It was only a boring afternoon variety-entertainment program anyway. Droning on about hyped-up stupid gossip. Besides, I've got nothing else to do. And it's not like I don't feel guilty about still living at home with no job at the age of thirty. The least I can do is play along with Mom's transparent ploy to get me out of the house.

"Oh, that's a big help," she says brightly.

I stand up and she shoots her hand out at me with the folded-up eco bag in it.

"Daikon and taro. Oh, and bananas too."

Woah, easy does it… But I say nothing as I stuff the bag and my wallet in my jacket pocket and head out.

I reach the front gate of the school and find it closed. Seems like the Community House has a different entrance. There's a signboard and I follow it around to a white building. I enter through the glass front door. An old guy with thick gray hair is sitting at a desk in the office behind a narrow front desk. He comes to the window and points to a form in a plastic binder on the counter.

"Write your name and purpose of visit here, please. And the time."

The heading on the form says "Visitors' Log."

I clock Mom's name there and some others. They wrote *market* so that's what I write too, next to my name, Hiroya Suda.

The market is in the lobby. The space is not big but they have a whole lot of tables spread with things for sale. Vegetables, fruit, bread. Not many customers, though. I move swiftly around and collect all the items on my list.

I spy a whiteboard in one corner with the word "Register" on it. Aha, this is where I go to pay. Two ladies stand next to it, yakking away. One wears an Agricultural Co-op sweatshirt and the other a red bandana around her hair. I head over with my arms full of daikon, taro and bananas and dump them on a table. Then I go to pull out my wallet, and something catches my eye next to the handwritten "Welcome" sign.

"Monger!"

The ladies turn to look at me.

I'd spotted Monger, a character from the Fujiko F. Fujio manga series *21 Emon*. Monger has a round, squat body and a pointy head, like a chestnut, with a curl of hair at the top. I reach out to touch the tiny stuffed toy about five centimeters high but Red Bandana stops me.

"Sorry, that's not for sale. It's one of Sayuri's felted mascots. She gave it to me when I borrowed a book."

"Sayuri?"

"Sayuri Komachi, in the library. That's who made it."

The manga artist duo Fujiko Fujio is famous for creating *Doraemon* and other works, but *21 Emon* is not famous. It's a futuristic sci-fi story about Emon, a kid who inherits a run-down inn that's been in his family for centuries. I think it's their best work, but I'm in the minority. That's why this girl, Sayuri Komachi, sounds interesting. What's she like? I wouldn't mind having a look at her.

I shove the taro and bananas in the eco bag and stick the great big daikon under my arm, then get directions for the library. It's at the back of the building—easy enough to find.

First I stand in the doorway to check out the scene. At the front desk a girl with a ponytail is very carefully scanning barcodes from a big pile of books. So this is Sayuri Komachi. Interesting. She's younger than I expected. Probably still a teenager. Very cute, though. Petite, big round eyes. She's like a squirrel. Damn—I can't help giving a stupid smile.

Time to prep myself. *Okay, this is a library. It's free, anyone can enter. Go.* I take a deep breath and edge in, but Sayuri catches wind of me. Uh-oh. Her head bobs up and she looks at me. My feet stop.

"Hello." She smiles.

"Uh, hi," I mumble and keep moving.

The library is more compact than a normal city one.

I reach the stacks and find myself surrounded by rows of bookshelves. Nostalgia washes over me. This place has atmosphere, different from a bookshop with just new books. In here you sense the weight of time, stretching way back to the past. I rotate my body 360 degrees to absorb it all.

After a while I summon the courage to speak to Sayuri. "Um, have you got manga?"

She grins at me. "Yes, we do. Just a few."

Fearlessly, I continue. "Do you like *21 Emon?*"

"*21 Emon?*"

"Yeah, by Fujiko Fujio."

Sayuri looks confused. "I know *Doraemon*, but…" She smiles apologetically.

Huh. That's what most people say. I never understand. "But you made Monger for the lady at the market," I blurt in disappointment.

Sayuri nods. "You mean the mascot Mrs. Muroi is so fond of? Ms. Komachi, the librarian, made that. You'll find her in the reference corner at the back. She can probably recommend some manga for you, too."

Ding! A new bell rings in my heart. Now I get it— the library has more than one member of staff. Then I see the name tag around Ponytail Girl's neck, which was blocked by the pile of books until now. Her name is Nozomi Morinaga.

Hope bubbles like a spring in my chest as I head for

the reference corner. I locate it on the other side of a dual-purpose partition noticeboard. I inch toward the edge and peer around the corner. *Kyaah!* The sight of a humungous, fearsome woman squished behind the counter nearly causes my heart to stop. No way is this Sayuri Komachi! In great haste, I turn around and rush back to the front desk.

"Um, I didn't see anybody except someone who looks like Genma Saotome."

For a few seconds Nozomi says nothing. "Who's that?" she asks.

"Genma Saotome, in *Ranma ½*? You know, the one who turns into a giant panda when water splashes on him."

"A person who turns into a panda? That sounds fun."

Not. Genma Saotome is one friggin' tough, unfriendly giant panda. I wish I could explain this to her.

"So is that Ms. Komachi in there? Who makes the stuffed animals?"

"Yes, it is. She's really good with her hands."

Aha. Now I get it. I had it fixed in my head that a girl made the Monger toy, because of Red Bandana calling her Sayuri, but if Genma Saotome made it, that too could be interesting. Maybe I *can* talk to her.

"I'll look after your things. Please, go and consult her."

Nozomi smiles and holds her hands out to me. How can I say no? I hand her my eco bag and daikon, then return to the reference corner. At second glance, I confirm that the woman's name tag reads "Sayuri Komachi." Her hands move and she is in a state of deep concentration. I inch forward and observe that she appears to be making a tiny stuffed animal. She stabs a needle into a ball of wool placed on a square foam mat. This action is repeated over and over. Is that how she makes the toys?

Suddenly, she stops and turns to look at me. Man, her eyes are scary.

"What are you looking for?"

Her voice is deep and low. I gulp. What am I looking for? Words spring into my mind and take me by surprise. Tears form.

"I'm looking for...uh, yeah, that's right... I'm looking for..."

Oh crap. Why am I blubbering? I wipe my palm over my cheek.

Ms. Komachi is unmoved. She looks down and begins stabbing with the needle again. "Rumi Takahashi is rather good, don't you think?"

Uh-oh, she heard me earlier. Rumi Takahashi is the creator of *Ranma ½*. I probably offended her by calling her Genma Saotome.

"Um, yes."

"*Urusei Yatsura* and *Maison Ikkoku* are good too, but I think I like the *Mermaid Saga* series most."

"Me too! Me too!"

We start jawing about our favorite manga. *The Drifting Classroom* by Kazuo Umezu, *Master Keaton* by Naoki Urasawa and *Emperor of the Land of the Rising Sun* by Ryoko Yamagishi. To name but a few. Ms. Komachi knows every title I mention. She doesn't say much. Just works on her soft toy the whole time, giving spot-on comments every now and then.

After a while she stops and opens an orange box in front of her. I recognize the honeycomb and white flower pattern. It's a box of Kuremiyado Honeydome soft cookies. Everybody knows these. My grandma used to love them and they always appear at family gatherings. Grandma always said they were delicious and easy to chew.

I thought Ms. Komachi would offer me a Honeydome cookie, but she doesn't. The box is for storing her toy-making gear. She must like recycling things. She sticks the needle into a pincushion, closes the lid and looks at me with laser eyes.

"For someone so young, you certainly know the old manga."

"My uncle had a manga café. I used to hang out there when I was at elementary school."

A manga café is not like the internet cafés of today. Basically it's a coffee shop with heaps of manga. They were common when I was a kid. They don't have private rooms, just tables where you can sit and order a drink, then read from the manga library in the shop.

My mother went out to work when I was eight, so after school I used to ride my bike for twenty minutes to the Kitami Manga Café run by my uncle and aunt. They let me stay as long as I liked, and served me drinks while I read manga. I never paid for the drinks but I'm pretty sure Mom settled up later. I'd hang out there until she finished work, and read from their huge collection. That's how I met my childhood friends, in all the manga I read.

I began to draw them and became obsessed with illustrating. After high school I went to design school to study it, but couldn't find a job. There was no place where I could do the kind of illustration work I liked, and I didn't know how to go about applying for other kinds of jobs. I had nothing going for me except my ability to draw, and if I couldn't even find a job doing that, then I didn't know how I could be capable of doing anything else. In the end I never found a proper job, and I never managed to stick with all the part-time ones I tried. So here I am at thirty, still a NEET.

"Manga artists are incredible. I thought illustrating would be a cool thing to do and went to vocational school. Then I discovered I didn't have what it took to make it as an artist."

This is the pathetic excuse I give for being unemployed.

Ms. Komachi rolls her head around and clicks her neck. "Why is that?" Her head tilts to one side.

"Because only the chosen few can make a living from illustrating. Not just illustrating either—probably less than one person in a hundred can turn the thing they like doing into paid work."

Ms Komachi rolls her head again and lifts an index finger. "I'm going to give you a math lesson."

"What?"

"In the case of one hundred people, one person out of a hundred is one per cent, correct?"

"Yeah."

"But in the case of one person doing the thing they want to do, there is only yourself, which means one person out of one, which is one hundred percent."

"Huh?"

"So there's a hundred percent chance."

"Uh…"

This does not sound right. Is it some kind of trick? But Ms. Komachi's expression does not change. She still looks dead serious and scary. She is not joking.

"Let's see."

She straightens up and turns to face her computer. Then suddenly she launches into pounding the keyboard with incredible speed. *Tatatatatatatataa!*

"Are you Kenshiro?!"

I can't help myself. She is just like Kenshiro in *Fist of the North Star* unleashing his killer technique on an enemy by attacking at high speed with supreme skill.

Ms. Komachi says nothing. After a final *ta!* she sits up. The printer begins to whir.

"You are already living," she growls in a threatening voice when she hands me the sheet of paper from the printer. It sends shivers up my spine. I recognize the parody of Kenshiro's catchphrase: "You are already dead."

The printout has one line of writing on it. A book called *Evolution: A Visual Record* with the author's name and the shelf number.

"Uh, what's this manga?"

"There is no manga I could recommend to you. Nothing that could surpass the wealth of treasures you accumulated in your childhood."

She begins to search through the fourth drawer below the counter. I watch and wonder what she is doing. Suddenly she reaches across and hands me something.

"This one's for you. Please take it. It's a bonus gift with the book."

It feels soft. Hope rises in my chest. Is it a Monger? But no, my hopes are dashed. It's a plane. A plane with a tiny gray body, white wings and a cool green tail.

I'm lost for words but it doesn't matter. Ms. Komachi has already opened the Honeydome box and is busy making her stuffed toy again. The sour look has returned to her face. Moments earlier she had been giving me her complete attention, but now it's like she has completely closed down. As if someone had flicked a switch.

There is nothing more for me to say, so I take the printout and go to look for the book. I find it in natural sciences, close to the reference corner. A large, heavy, illustrated book.

The front cover has a photograph of a silver bird against a black background. A close-up shot, taken side on from the neck upward, clearly showing tufts of eyelashes sprouting above the bird's large eyes, and its hard beak tapering to a point. It reminds me of a beautiful exotic model, or the bird in Osamu Tezuka's famous *Phoenix* manga.

The title *Evolution: A Visual Record* is in large black lettering.

The book is large and bulky, too big to read standing up, so I crouch down and open it. The first half has long sections of text, but the rest is mostly a collection of incredible photographs. There are photos of birds, reptiles, plants and insects. Every single one is a work of art. They blow my mind. They are so intense...and colorful. And all perfectly composed. They have a kind of spooky aura as well. This is so weird. I have no idea why Ms. Komachi recommended this book, but I like it. I really like it. These images from real life could be straight out of a fantasy world.

"Shall I make a borrower's card for you? If you live in the ward, you're entitled to one," Nozomi calls out to me as she passes by to reshelve a book.

"Uh, no…but… It's too heavy to take home. Anyway, I've got the daikon and stuff to carry."

"Why don't you come here and read it?" A voice from behind me shoots back. It's Ms. Komachi. I turn around to see her, her gaze boring into me.

"I'll label it 'on loan' and hold it for you. Come back and read it whenever you like."

I stare up at her from my crouching position. There are no words I can say. Relief, happiness, emotions I have no label for, overwhelm me. I almost start blubbering again. It's okay. It's okay for me to be in this place.

"It will take you quite a while to read it all." Ms. Komachi pulls her lips sideways into a smile.

My head nods mechanically.

~

The next day is Saturday and I have a train to catch. I haven't done that for a very long time, but today is my high-school reunion. Normally I would not attend but I cannot miss this one. A time capsule that was buried in the school grounds on the day we all graduated will be dug up this year. The year we all turn thirty.

When I received the invitation and read, "The organizer will post time capsule contributions for anyone who can't make it on the day," a chill ran down my spine. If the pieces of paper were sealed in envelopes it might be okay, but I remember how we just folded them up and wrote our names on the back. Anybody could easily look to see what was written on them.

My mission for today is to retrieve my piece of paper without anyone else seeing it. I will not attend the party afterward. Not a hope.

In the last year of high school, thirty seemed like centuries away. So old and adult. I thought all my problems would be solved by then. In my final year, I was just happy to be finishing and going off to study illustration. Never again would I have to suffer through gym or math classes, or anything else I was no good at. All I would do from then on was draw. Nothing else. I was also living with the fantasy that my path to a career as an illustrator was already laid out.

I will become an illustrator whose name will be remembered in history. I'm pretty sure that's what I wrote. It makes me cringe to think about it now.

I didn't write that because I was superconfident about my talent, or a single-minded, deadly ambitious type. It was just heat of the moment. Youthful indiscretion and getting carried away by the occasion. But I did think I would be doing *something* by the time I was thirty. Even if I wasn't famous. Some kind of job close to what I wanted to be doing.

~

After twelve years, here I am back at school again. A crowd is already gathered next to the large beech tree in a corner of the grounds where the time capsule is buried. A plastic post shaped like a grave marker, with "17th Graduating Class Time Capsule" written on it, marks the spot near its roots. Sugimura, our former class rep and today's organizer, stands next to it holding a big shovel. He wears an expensive down jacket over a sharp-looking shirt.

As I approach, a few people turn to look at me and nod or wave. But that's all. Every single one goes straight back to talking with whoever is next to them. I guess nobody remembers me.

I hang around by the tree, watching the scene. Then somebody calls my name from behind. I turn around and see a short, skinny guy. It's Seitaro. We weren't close buddies or anything, but I did use to talk with him sometimes. He was quiet and always had his nose in a book. Not the type to hang out with anyone. We exchanged New Year's greeting cards a few times after leaving school, so that's how I know he went to university and then got a job in the Waterworks Bureau.

Seitaro gives me a friendly smile. "You look well."

"You too, Seitaro," I say and look down, so he'll get the idea I don't want to answer any more questions. Especially about what I do.

Two guys come up to us. One is called Nishiya, but I can't remember the name of his sidekick. They were the loudest boys in our class. I never had a proper conversation with either.

"Hey, if it isn't Seitaro." Nishiya speaks with a sneer. He shoots me a glance, but ignores me. I don't interest him apparently. I turn away from him.

Sugimura calls for everybody's attention. "Okay, we're all here now—let's get started!"

The crowd pushes in all at once. Everybody watches with bated breath while the soil, after twelve years, is finally dug up. Before long we hear the sound of the shovel hitting metal. Sugimura brushes away dirt with gloved hands and reveals a dull silver object wrapped in plastic. The rice cracker tin containing the messages to our future selves was sealed with tape and placed in a plastic bag. The crowd cheers as it is lifted clear of the dirt.

Sugimura carefully peels off the tape and opens the lid.

Inside is a jumble of yellowing pieces of paper, all folded differently. One by one, he pulls them from the tin and reads the names before handing them out. Some people snicker to themselves when they read what they wrote. Others show their neighbors and elbow each other, and some just read it out loud on the spot. The messages range from future dreams, to confessions of love, or beefs the writer had but was never able to say out loud.

Everybody is looking confident and animated. All having a great time. By the age of thirty, things have fallen into place for most people. They're more or less settled, with jobs and families. Nobody here today is a student anymore. This is a bunch of adults who've shed their school uniforms and evolved into something else.

Finally, my name is called. I take the piece of paper from Sugimura and immediately shove it straight into my jacket pocket. Task accomplished. I don't even want to look at it. At last I can relax.

Seitaro's turn is next. He opens his piece of paper delicately.

"Oooh, famous writer, are we?" Nishiya sticks his beak over Seitaro's shoulder to look. The words "I will become a writer" are written neatly in the center of the sheet.

"You always used to send stuff off to magazines, didn't ya, Seitaro. So did ya write yer novel yet?" Nishiya asks.

"Yes, I did," Seitaro replies without hesitation.

"Huh. When was it published?"

Sidekick butts in to say, "What? *You* published a book?"

"I haven't been published yet. But I still write." Seitaro smiles timidly.

Nishiya bares his teeth in a grin. "Aren't you the one. Still chasing dreams at this age."

Losing my temper with a snap, I glare at Nishiya. In my head, I begin to rant: *Quit that! Apologize to Seitaro for making fun of him. Seitaro's novels are wicked. I like them. How would you know anyway? Who do you think you are saying that? Making fun of somebody who's trying their best— that really sucks. Back off!*

Nishiya and Sidekick pay my silent dirty looks no heed. They move on to a group of three girls nearby and start joshing with them.

Seitaro let me read a novel of his once when we were at school. He came up quietly during recess one day as I was drawing and looked at what I'd done. "That's fantastic," he'd said. I think he really might've been impressed. Then he showed me his notebook and asked, "Would you mind reading my novel?"

To tell the truth, I can't remember what it was about. But I do remember I was massively impressed.

"I'm leaving," I say, and walk off.

Seitaro comes after me. "Wait. Let's go together."

"You had enough? What about the party?"

Seitaro shakes his head in reply. "I'm not going either."

Nobody pays us any attention as we peel away from the buzzing crowd and exit through the school gates. On the way to the station, we talk about nothing much. *That beech tree had grown a lot, hadn't it? It was a warm winter this year...* Stuff like that. Then we pass by a Mister Donut and Seitaro suddenly turns to me: "Hey, do you want to get a coffee?"

He's got this embarrassed smile on his face that makes me blush with embarrassment too. We both look the other way as we nod and awkwardly go inside. We order drinks and find a table.

"You were really good at drawing, Hiroya. Didn't you go to design school?" Seitaro asks as he sits down opposite me.

"Yeah." I reply after a beat. "But it didn't work out. My drawings weren't what people wanted. Even at design school I was always being told they were too bizarre, or niche."

"What! I'm the opposite. People always say my novels are too ordinary. Too bland, no spice. Whenever I got selected for feedback in any competitions I've entered—and I've entered a lot—that's the kind of comment I always get." Seitaro smiles, as if he enjoys saying this about himself. He takes a sip of his latte.

"But you kept on writing anyway, didn't you? That's great."

"Yeah. I focus on my writing in the evening and at weekends. Weekdays I have to work."

This makes sense. He might not be doing his ideal job, but he makes a living and is still chasing his dream. I have a lot of respect for Seitaro.

"I guess working at the Waterworks Bureau is a secure job." Even as I say it, I'm thinking what a cliché that is.

Seitaro clasps his cup in both hands. "What kind of job do you think is totally secure?" he quizzes me in return.

"A public employee like you, or a big corporation?"

"Nothing is," he replies, gently shaking his head. "Not one single job I could name is absolutely secure. Everybody just does their best to hang in there, trying to balance it all."

His expression is mild, but his tone is dead serious.

"There's no guarantee of certainty in anything. But the flip side to there being no guarantee of security, is that there's also no certainty that something is a dud." Seitaro bites his lip.

I get it. I understand why Seitaro sticks with what he likes doing. Nishiya's words from earlier flash through my mind and I clench my fists in anger.

"Seitaro, you have to get published. To make Nishiya eat dirt."

Seitaro laughs softly and shakes his head again.

"People who make fun of me now won't stop, no matter

what the future brings. They'll always find some angle to attack me with. But don't worry, I'm okay with it. I don't care what people who've never read my novels think."

He gulps down his coffee and gives me a firm look in the eye.

"I don't have it in me to get my own back or use anger as a tool for revenge. It's something else that motivates me, something completely different."

There's a gleam in Seitaro's eyes as he speaks. Seitaro is a skinny guy. Everything about him is thin and delicate. His neck, his fingers, even his hair. He may look mild on the outside, but inside he's steel. Whatever inside that skinny body is driving him, I'm jealous of it.

I choose my next words with care. "Seitaro, don't you worry sometimes you might get old without ever getting your novels published?"

His eyeballs roll to the corners, like he's digging through the files in his brain. Then he speaks. "It's not like I'm not worried, but Haruki Murakami debuted at thirty. Knowing that kept me going all through my twenties."

"Uh-huh."

"But when it started looking like I couldn't count on that, I panicked and looked around for another role model. Jiro Asada made his debut at forty."

"Great. So you got a ten-year reprieve."

Seitaro laughs. "If I miss that deadline there are probably others. There's no age limit on a writing debut. I figure everybody has their own personal timing that works best for them." Then he blushes.

When Seitaro asks me to exchange LINE IDs with him, I install the LINE messaging app on my smartphone for the very first time.

~

The next day I head over to the Community House library, as Ms. Komachi suggested. It's quiet, mostly empty apart from one or two elderly people.

When I arrive, Ms. Komachi pulls out *Evolution: A Visual Record* and puts it on the counter without a word. It has an "OUT ON LOAN" label wrapped around it, held in place with a rubber band. I guess this means I can come and look at it whenever I want. I lift the book off the counter with a nod and take it over to the reading table.

When I open it and turn to the introduction, "Darwin, Wallace, and the Birth of a Theory," I do a double take. It's about natural selection and how the theory was born. I learned a bit about this at school. Creatures that adapt to their environment survive, while those that cannot adapt become extinct. That's basically the idea. One sentence really depresses me, though: "Favorable variations would tend to be preserved, and unfavorable ones to be destroyed."

Favorable and unfavorable. What am I supposed to make of that? I've never heard of Wallace but the more I read about him the more my gut churns. My eyes move closer and closer to the page.

When people hear the phrase 'theory of evolution' they usually think of Darwin. The same Charles Darwin who wrote *On the Origin of Species*. But I was learning that someone else discovered it, too, a man called Alfred Russell Wallace, also a natural historian and fourteen years younger than Darwin. Their personalities and situation in life were very different—Darwin had money, Wallace not so much. But both were nuts about beetle research and, independently, both hit on a theory of evolution through natural selection. In those days, though, everybody believed absolutely in creation, as described in the Bible, and that everything in this world was the work of the Lord. Anyone who said otherwise had better watch out.

That's why Darwin was scared about going public with his theory. Wallace wasn't, though; Wallace just kept on writing and publishing. So then Darwin started to panic. He knew that if he didn't want to lose all credit for a theory he had thought about for so many years, he had to go public.

He bit the bullet and got on with getting *On the Origin of Species*—in a simplified version—ready for publication. ASAP. And to this day, everybody has heard of this book and Darwin.

The more I read, the more irritated I become. Then I reach a part where Wallace says about Darwin, "We were good friends."

I shake my head. *You sure about that, Wallace?*

Wallace published first, but Darwin is the name everybody remembers. This does not sit right with me. Something similar happened to me at design school. There was a guy who always used to sneak a look at my drawings and then copy the composition or particular details. His work got all the praise, though, because he was much better at drawing than me, even if the designs were my idea in the first place. I used to get so mad and stewed over it a lot, but never told anybody. If I'd said, "But I thought of it, too," nobody would've believed me. The golden boy always wins. Always.

I sigh deeply and turn the page. Then I see a full-page photo of the skeleton of a fossilized bird. A magnificently preserved specimen. According to the caption, it's called a *Confuciusornis*, and it lived in the Early Cretaceous period. It looks like it's asleep, with wings spread wide and beak half open. I gawk at it in amazement, absorbing all the detail. Then *Whoa!* All of a sudden I get the urge to draw. I haven't felt this in ages. I know I won't be able to settle until I do something about it.

I remember the piece of paper stuck between the pages. The one that was wrapped around the book when Ms. Komachi handed it to me. Then I go and borrow a ballpoint pen from Nozomi. Now I have everything I need: a black pen and a white sheet of paper.

I take my time and stare at the *Confuciusornis* to study every angle. Then slowly I start to draw an image. Time melts away. The outline of a bird emerges from the tip of my pen. My imagination soars and the bones become a living thing. Before I know it, the bird has sprung to life. This ugly, grotesque creature has a deep-seated moral code and sense of justice. I give it sharp scythes on the tips of its wings for slashing at the forces of evil, and tiny goldfish to live in the hollows of its eyes.

I'm so lost in my own world that when Nozomi squeals loudly at my elbow, I nearly jump out of my skin. I cringe, waiting for the inevitable. She's gonna say *Gross!* I just know it.

But she doesn't. Her eyes sparkling, she calls out, "Ms. Komachi, come and look at this! Hiroya's done a lovely drawing!"

Hiroya? She said my name? She must've remembered it from when she made the borrower's card. And…she praised my drawing!

Ms. Komachi emerges from behind the counter. She walks over with a graceful rolling motion and examines the drawing. Then she makes a strange throat-clearing sound, nods and says, "Wonderful originality."

"You should enter it for a contest or something," Nozomi chimes in.

What can I say? I grope for the right words. "Nah, I'd have no chance."

I go to screw up the paper, but Nozomi stops me. "Wait. If you're throwing it away, can I have it?" she says.

"You sure? You don't think it's grotesque?"

"It's good," she insists, and snatches the paper away from me, holding it to her chest with both hands. "Yes it's grotesque, sure, but funny too, and lovable in its own way."

Zowee! Somebody gets it! Of course she's only saying this to be nice, though. I'm not fooled.

In any case, Nozomi has saved the skeleton bird's life. It feels like a sign. Maybe this will work out after all. Maybe I can come back tomorrow. My cheek muscles relax into a smile.

~

Next day, just as I'm about to enter the library, I run into Bandana Lady from the market. The one called Mrs. Muroi. She's wiping the banisters with a cleaning cloth.

"Hello," she says. "It's Sayuri's day off today."

"Ah, I didn't know."

Then I remember; she's the reason I went to the library in the first place.

"You called her Sayuri that time, so I thought she was a girl."

Mrs. Muroi laughs loudly. "For someone my age, which is sixty-two," she says, "Sayuri *is* young. She's only forty-seven, you know."

Forty-seven? That's young? I'm thirty but already I feel old. But young and old might be relative. Age doesn't seem relevant to Ms. Komachi, somehow. She's just a person, which is a pretty obvious thing to say, I suppose.

"So, do you like Monger?"

"Monger!" Mrs. Muroi suddenly yells, making me jump, and laughs again. "I love Monger. The ultimate creature!"

She's right about that. Monger is not much to look at, but he's the ultimate creature. He can endure extreme cold and scorching heat, eat anything as a source of energy, and he can teleport.

"He might be tough enough to survive any conditions and have special powers, but he sulks if he doesn't get enough attention and cries at the drop of a hat. It makes you wonder what strength really is, doesn't it?"

This feels like she might be saying something deep, so I keep my mouth shut.

"When Sayuri first came to work here around three years ago, I told her I liked Monger. Then one day when I went to consult her about cookbooks, she gave me a handmade felted mascot with the books. Such a sweet thing to do. So I told her it was a wonderful bonus gift to go with the books. She seemed to like that expression."

"So, you're good friends with Ms. Komachi?"

Mrs. Muroi nods, then squats down to rinse the cloth in a bucket of water. "But I'm leaving at the end of March," she says, looking up at me with a proud smile. "My daughter's having a baby in April and I'll be a grandma. I'm quitting so I can help her out for a while. Someone new is taking over from me at the beginning of the new fiscal year in April."

Apparently work contracts at the Community House are awarded for a year at a time, but can be renewed if both sides agree.

"I'm only here for another month, but I'll see you around," she says, picking up the bucket to leave.

~

When I enter the library, Nozomi welcomes me with a grin. There is no sign of Ms. Komachi, as Mrs. Muroi said, but *Evolution: A Visual Record* is on top of the reference counter with a rubber band around it. Obviously left out for me in case I come in again. Like yesterday, it's quiet, with few people around, and I have the reading table all to myself when I sit down and open the book.

I made my way through "Ancient History," "Birds" and "Diversity in Cold Blood." Now I'm in the plants chapter, deeply engrossed in a dewy Venus flytrap, when suddenly I get a feeling of being watched. I look up and see Nozomi's eyes on me. My own widen and she smiles at me easily in return. My heart starts thumping.

"Useless, aren't I, sitting here looking at photos of a Venus flytrap at my age instead of being out at work," I say clumsily. I'm not used to this.

Nozomi shakes her head, still smiling.

"Uh-uh. Looking at you, Hiroya, reminds me of when I was at elementary school. I used to go to the nurse's room instead of the classroom, you know. It's not quite the same, but I think you get it."

The nurse's room? Nozomi? Who would've thought?

"Ms. Komachi used to be the special-needs teacher at the school next door, where I went to school. There was a period when I couldn't enter the classroom, so I used to go to the nurse's room instead, every day."

Now she mentions it, I remember Nozomi referring once to Ms. Komachi as her teacher. I'd thought it was because she's teaching Nozomi how to be a librarian, but in fact she was Nozomi's teacher from elementary school.

"Why couldn't you go into the classroom?"

Nozomi laughs. "I guess I couldn't be like everybody else."

I could say the same about me. But it's not something I can talk about casually, so instead I just nod.

"I was afraid of loud voices. But kids that age are always loud, aren't they? Laughing and shouting randomly. If the teacher told the other kids off, I felt like I was to blame too, and I was always on edge. Kids pick up on that kind of thing. They can sense when someone's different, or delicate. It wasn't that I was actually bullied so much as sort of ignored. I began to feel like I had no right to be in the classroom."

I can see from the way she says this, in a brittle, bright tone, what a tough time she'd had.

"So when I couldn't even enter my own classroom anymore, Mom talked with my class teacher and it was decided I could go to the nurse's room instead. The first time I visited, Miss—er, Ms. Komachi—happened to say something that really made a difference to me. She told me that a reading report I'd done for summer holiday homework was very interesting. Apparently she'd read it on the noticeboard in the corridor. I knew she wasn't lying because she told me exactly which parts were good and why. It made me feel so good about myself that every

217

time I read a book after that, I wrote a report and gave it to Ms. Komachi to look at."

Nozomi pauses and looks at the shelves of books around her.

"Over time, I gradually got my confidence back to return to the classroom. When I went to high school, Ms. Komachi started working here as a librarian, so when I finished school I asked her for advice about becoming one myself. She recommended that I work here as a library assistant."

"Library assistant?"

"Yes. If you take a library assistant short training course, as I did, then work for three years, you can qualify for the librarian training course."

"So you need three years' experience as an assistant librarian first?"

"Yes, if you're a high-school graduate. You can also go to university to study but my family can't afford it. Besides, I wanted to work in a library straight away."

She has a long road ahead. Becoming a librarian is harder than I thought.

"You're lucky, though, that you knew what you wanted to do at such a young age, and you started on that path straight away."

"But you're the same, aren't you, Hiroya? You went to design school straight from high school."

"Yeah, but nobody likes my work. My drawings are too dark and creepy."

Nozomi's head suddenly tips to one side. A bit like the way Ms. Komachi's does. "Uh-huh, uh-huh," she mumbles, rolling her eyes around as if thinking something over. Suddenly she turns to me and cries, "Sweet-and-sour pork!"

"What?"

"What do you think about pineapple in sweet-and-sour pork?"

I stare at her in confusion.

Red faced, she begins explaining: "A lot of people don't like it, do they? They can't stand pineapple in sweet-and-sour pork. But it never disappears, does it? Why is that?"

"Er, I don't know—why doesn't it?"

"Because the people who like pineapple in sweet-and-sour pork may be in a minority, but they don't just *like* it, they're *crazy* about it. It's a question of passion. The majority may not accept something, but as long as there are some who do, the existence of that thing—whatever it may be—is protected. I like it," she adds, "pineapple in sweet-and-sour pork, that is. And the picture you drew."

I don't know what to say. Except, maybe... *Yowee!* "Like" is a great word—one that can save people. Somebody likes me, and my pictures. Even if she was just being nice.

~

On my way home, I feel like I'm walking on air. But when I arrive, Mom is on the phone, deep in conversation. Instantly I know who's on the other end. Her bright voice is a dead giveaway.

"Your brother's coming back to Japan in April!" she tells me happily as she hangs up.

All of a sudden, I feel the air sucked out of my lungs. Her voice pings in my brain.

"He's been assigned back to the Tokyo head office to join a new department."

I knew this day would come. "Oh, nice," I say, and head for the bathroom so she won't see how upset I am.

~

Water splashes everywhere as I scrub my hands vigorously and wash my face. One line from the evolution book keeps running through my brain: "Favorable variations would tend to be preserved, and unfavorable ones to be destroyed."

Big Bro the achiever. Huh. He's always been that way, ever since we were kids. We may be related but I'm nothing like him. I was always the timid, anxious type.

He was in middle school and I was in elementary

when Mom and Dad split up. The two of us stayed with Mom, and he started studying harder than ever. He always looked angry. Maybe he was mad at Dad, or at the way our situation sucked. I don't know. But whatever it was, if I ever spoke to him, he'd just look at me like I was an insect. Home was too small and cramped and I didn't want to get in his way. That's why I used to go to Kitami Manga Café after school. But then we moved to Tokyo, where it was easier for Mom to find work with hours that fitted in with raising children on her own. So that was the end of the manga café for me.

Eventually he won a scholarship to university and, after graduating, joined a trading company and Mom was able to quit full-time work. It had been really tough for her, so she was glad to switch to a part-time position at her favorite bakery instead.

Four years ago, Big Bro was posted to Germany, and I have to say I was glad. When he's around, I can't help feeling like the worst example of a human being ever. But I tried, I really did. I did my best to find a job, but I just couldn't pull it off.

After design school, I found a position as a sales rep in a company that made educational materials for crammers and home study. During the day I went out and did the rounds and at the end of it I made phone calls.

But I'm not good at talking, and all I ever did was get under people's skin. It made me feel like shit. I could never achieve my quotas, and my boss was always mad at me. *If you really wanted to do it, you could*, he'd say, or *You're totally useless*. Shit like that.

After a month, my body refused to move. I couldn't make myself get out of bed. If I did manage to drag myself to the front door, just trying to put my shoes on would freeze my brain. My whole body would go rigid and tears dripped from my eyes like a leaky tap. The more I tried to make myself move, the more my body just seized up. I was a total mess. I just couldn't function anymore. So I quit. And, I'm embarrassed to say, Mom did all the paperwork for me. I'm such a deadbeat, I couldn't even do that for myself.

I had some time off for a while and then I thought I should at least look for part-time work. But in all the convenience stores or fast-food joints, you have to be able to do a lot of tasks fast and at the same time. I used to make so many mistakes that all I did was cause trouble and never lasted more than two weeks. Then I tried working for a removal company, but could barely stand up after the first day, so I quit the next.

There's probably no job on earth that I'm capable of doing.

~

Mom looks on top of the world. And why wouldn't she? Her talented, dependable, successful son is coming home. Returning from a distant country by plane— something I've never even been on. And now she's talking about us going to meet him at the airport. Uh-uh. Not a chance.

In this family he's the one who evolved. I'm the unfavorable variation.

~

I remember the plane Ms. Komachi gave me. A long time ago, people probably used to look up at the sky, see birds flying and think how they'd like to fly too. They would've known, though, that no matter how highly evolved humans might be, they can't grow feathers. I suppose that's how they came to build planes.

I'll never be a bird, or build a plane. I'll never be able to fly.

~

What are you looking for?
When Ms. Komachi asked me this question, my first

thought was: *I'm still searching.* Searching for somewhere I can be accepted as I am. Just one place is all I need. Somewhere to be at peace.

~

Next day, I enter the library and blink when I see Ms. Komachi filling out the space behind the counter for checkouts and returns. Today must be Nozomi's day off. The Honeydome box is there and Ms. Komachi is stabbing away at a soft toy as usual.

I collect my book and head straight for the reading table, muttering under my breath (or so I thought), "She must really love that." But she must have heard me.

"I had a student once who used to do this in the nurse's room," Ms. Komachi says, without lifting her eyes from her hands. "At first I assumed she simply enjoyed handicrafts, but after watching her I realized it was something else. I saw that concentrating on poking a needle into a ball of wool is hypnotic. When I tried it for myself, I found that any feelings of agitation or disquiet would gradually calm down and settle. And I realized that this was a means to find a sense of balance. I learned something very useful."

Did I hear right? Ms. Komachi has feelings of anxiety and agitation? She always looks as if nothing could fluster her.

I sit down and open up the *Evolution* book, and the churning in my gut from yesterday's news begins to fade. Ms. Komachi's presence close by is comforting. Her hands move constantly, and though she appears to have no particular interest in me, I don't feel rejected. I'm grateful. Not least for her telling me I can come here anytime to read.

But I can't spend the rest of my life in here reading books. Kids eventually leave school and move on to the next thing, but I don't have any specific milestone in my future that will automatically come around. And nobody to decide when something should start or finish.

Creatures that can't adapt to the environment cease to exist. That's what natural selection is. In that case, I wish I could just be wiped off the face of the earth. No more life of pain, knowing I can't adapt, knowing people think I'm a useless mutant. I might not be the biggest talent, but if I just had a scrap of what it takes to get on in the world, I might be able to make a go of it, even if it did mean playing it a bit dirty sometimes. But I can't do it.

What did Wallace *really* think about Darwin? Did he genuinely regard Darwin as a "good friend"? Despite not receiving any glory for the theory of evolution?

I feel an overwhelming sense of suffocation. The pain felt by anyone, anywhere, who has ever been kicked aside. I lay my head down on the still-open book.

"What's wrong?" Ms. Komachi says flatly.

My brain struggles to find the words. "Darwin was a real prick, don't you think? I feel sorry for Wallace. Wallace was the first to try and publish, but Darwin got all the praise and attention. I'd never even heard of Wallace until I read this book."

Ms. Komachi says nothing. With my head still on the table, I picture her jabbing needle.

"You need to be careful when reading biographies and history."

I lift my head at this, and she looks me in the eye.

"You have to remember that it is merely one version of events, and only the parties involved can ever know the real truth. There are always numerous interpretations, and hearsay, about who said or did what. Misunderstandings occur even in real time; you can see that on the internet. So when it comes to events deep in the past, it's very difficult to be sure of what is accurate."

Her head leans to one side with a crack.

"But at least you know about Wallace now, don't you, Hiroya, from reading that book. Now he's in your thoughts, and you're making a place for him to live on in this world. Don't you think that's enough?"

I'm a place where Wallace lives on? Is that how you make a place for somebody—one person thinking about another?

"Besides, Wallace is respectably famous in his own right. The Wallace Line, for instance, that you see on world maps marking the distribution of fauna. I do think his achievements have been recognized. There must be so many other people who helped Wallace get where he did in life, who are also worthy of recognition but whose names have been lost." She puts an index finger to her forehead. "That aside, however, when I first read that *On the Origin of Species* was published only in 1859, my eyes nearly popped out of my head."

"Heh…how come?"

"Because it was a mere hundred and sixty years ago. That's very recent."

My brow wrinkles. One hundred and sixty years? Recent?

Ms. Komachi pats the flowery hairpin in her hair. "When you're close to fifty, one hundred years doesn't seem like an awfully long time. I almost feel I could live to a hundred and sixty if I try."

Put like that, maybe it's not so long. I wouldn't put it past Ms. Komachi to live to that age.

I hear her needle start to move again and look down at the book. This time I try to imagine all the people who might have been in Wallace's life, whose names are now lost to history.

~

As I leave the Community House, my smartphone rings. Seitaro's calling me. I almost never get calls from friends, and stop in my tracks nervously to take it.

"Hiroya... I... I..." Seitaro sounds like he's crying.

"Seitaro, hey, what's up?"

"I'm going to be published."

"What?"

"It's true. The end of last year I had an email from an editor at Maple Publications. Ms. Sakitani. She read a pamphlet I made for the autumn Literary Flea Market and wanted to meet me to discuss my novel. So we met a few times and I'm still working on polishing it, but today she got approval to schedule it for publication."

"Man, that's amazing! Seitaro, you rock!" I pump my fist. Seitaro's dream is coming true.

"I wanted to tell you first, Hiroya."

"No shit."

"You were the only one at school who ever said I could do it. You told me my novels were interesting, and I should keep writing. You've probably forgotten it, but I never did. It kept me going. Having somebody who believed in me was the best lucky charm ever."

Now I'm tearing up too. To think that one thing I said to him meant so much. But I know I'm not the only reason Seitaro kept on writing. Deep down, he also believes in himself.

"So, now you're an author, I guess you won't be working at the Waterworks Bureau anymore," I say with a sniff.

Seitaro laughs. "My job with the Waterworks Bureau is the reason I could keep writing. I'm not quitting."

I repeat his words in my head, and think about what it means. I can't explain it, but it makes sense.

"We'll have to celebrate," I say, before hanging up.

~

After Seitaro's call I can't settle, and agitatedly wander around outside the Community House until I find a small wooden bench near the steel fence to sit down. On the other side is the schoolyard, where kids play on the jungle gym at the end of the school day. The days are getting longer now, at the end of February. The school and Community House are supposedly joined, but only in name, it seems. From here, it looks like the school is not letting anyone into its grounds from the outside.

With my hands thrust into my jacket pockets, I take a few deep breaths to steady myself. My left hand clutches at the piece of paper from the time capsule, and my right one the toy plane Ms. Komachi gave me. Both have been sitting in my pockets all this time. I take them out and balance each on the palms of my hands.

I look at the plane first. People aren't astonished by airplanes anymore. They're an everyday sight. A convenience of civilization that everybody knows and accepts.

But only one hundred and sixty years ago, people in Europe were in no doubt that it was God who had made all creatures on earth, in exactly the form they were then. They had never looked any different and never would. People really did believe that salamanders were created from flames, and the bird of paradise was a messenger from paradise. That's why Darwin was reluctant to publish his theory. He was afraid of being shot down, for having an idea that didn't fit with the times and environment he lived in.

Now evolutionary theory is taken for granted. Something that used to be thought impossible is now common belief. Because Darwin, Wallace and other researchers who all believed in themselves kept on studying and publishing. Eventually they managed to make changes to their environment.

A hundred and sixty years ago, nobody would have believed this plane could ever exist. Metal is not supposed to fly.

All this time, I believed that I had no talent for drawing. I believed I could never have a normal working life.

Now I was starting to wonder. How much had my own thinking limited my opportunities?

The self I left behind in high school sits on the palm of my left hand. It had been preserved in dirt all these years. I open the piece of folded paper and give a start when I see the words I wrote.

I will draw art that people will remember...

Did I really write that? It's my handwriting, no mistake, so I must have. But at some point I became confused and misremembered the words. I was sure I'd written that my name would go down in history.

Poof! My vision of myself disintegrates. I've been playing the victim, a misfit with unrecognized talent in a society overrun by rapacious corporations. But all along, this is what my ambition had been.

I remember Nozomi's hand stopping me from screwing up the drawing. Her voice telling me she liked my pictures. At the time I thought she was just being polite; I didn't believe she was speaking truthfully. Because I don't believe in myself and I don't believe in other people.

I owe my eighteen-year-old self an apology. And it's not too late. There's still something I can do that's far more important than being remembered by history. And that is to draw. If I can draw just one picture that leaves a mark in somebody's life and is remembered, then I can find a place for me.

~

Next day I take my Croquis sketchbook and an assortment of pens and pencils with me to the Community House. A lot of the photos in *Evolution: A Visual Record* had been giving me the same kind of creative itch that *Confuciusornis* had. So now I planned to get myself properly reacquainted with the process of drawing. Just for the sake of it. I wouldn't even think about entering contests or anything.

I pass Ms. Komachi in the corridor, deep in conversation with the gray-haired man who's usually at the front desk.

Taking out *Evolution: A Visual Record* for myself, I settle down at the reading table and begin selecting photographs. Looking at them with a view to drawing produces a different kind of excitement in me. Should I use this North American longhorn beetle as the basis of a design? These bat wings might be a good starting point for a character. Or it might be interesting to draw a portrait of Wallace in pencil...

While I'm enthusiastically flipping through the pages, Ms. Komachi returns and I overhear her conversation with Nozomi.

"He said Mrs. Muroi can't work for quite a while."

I raise my head to look over at the counter.

"Her daughter's baby is coming earlier than expected. I'm sorry, Nozomi, but would you mind helping with the office cleaning until the end of March?"

Nozomi nods, but looks dismayed. I stand up. My body moves before my brain does.

"Um, I, er…"

Ms. Komachi turns around.

"Um, I, er… Maybe I could do it if you'd let me?"

Sweat breaks out on my forehead. Nozomi belongs in the library. She has to stay here, so she can become a librarian. She's trying so hard. I have no idea what this job involves, but at least I have the time to spare.

Ms. Komachi doesn't bat an eyelid. She gives me a long stare, then a faint smile forms on her lips.

∿

In the beginning it was tough to get here four times a week at eight-thirty in the morning. Not surprising, since I'd been in the habit of staying up until the early hours of the morning and then sleeping till noon every day. Not using an alarm clock to get up either. But I managed. Once I got through the tunnel of epic tiredness I felt every time the alarm went off, getting up and going outside would eventually make me fully awake. I was also so out of shape that the physical work was a shock to my body. But after a few days I was able to shake off the lethargy and became more energetic. Best of all was being paid money in exchange for my labor. It felt strange, after such a long time. I knew what I would do with my first paycheck.

The Community House has an upper floor where I'd never been before, with another reception area, a cleaner's room, computer room and an area for course information and support. There was enough space to hold dance lessons and seminars as well. Cleaning and managing equipment might be a job that even I can do, but it was a heck of a lot more work than I'd expected.

Ms. Komachi seemed to have spread the word that I could draw, and I began to get requests to do illustrations for the Community House newsletter and various posters. Sometimes I'd see people walk past them on the wall and stop to look or comment. Whenever I overheard praise, I'd do a secret fist pump inside. For some reason, little kids really seem to really like my illustrations.

Time in here passes at a slow, gentle pace. This is different to all the other part-time jobs I've had. I'm not useless. Perhaps my problem all along was not being in the right environment. One where I could make the most of myself. At the Community House, I feel useful. It's a huge relief. I have somewhere to be.

On the days when I have no shift, I go to the library

and draw. It's weird how ideas keep springing into my head now, as if a stopper has been removed. Yet when I had all the time in the world, I never had a single idea. I didn't even feel like drawing.

I see all kinds of people coming through here. The course instructors for color therapy sessions, arts and crafts workshops and various other events, plus all their students. I surprise myself at how sociable I can be, chatting with the ladies who come here regularly, and hitting it off with the little kids who come with their mothers.

Working here has given me a glimpse into how much thought and care goes into making life better for residents of the ward through this place. Somewhere they can feel safe and spend a bit of quality time, with opportunities for learning and entertainment. I'm learning stuff, too, from talking with the staff. The gray-haired man from reception is called Mr. Furuta. He's the facility director, employed by a foundation called the Ward Residents' Facilities Association, which is responsible for managing any ward facilities established by the Tokyo metropolitan government.

Before now I'd only ever thought about looking for work in companies and shops. I had no idea there were these other kinds of jobs in my neighborhood. It gives me hope to keep looking. There's a chance I might be able to find the perfect place for me after all.

I'm grateful for so many things. The chance to work here, a strong and healthy body that allows to me to do it, the smiles I get from people who come to the Community House. And my mother. Even when I quit the company, she never ever put any pressure on me, or blamed me. All these years while I was at home doing nothing, she kept encouraging me to get out, indirectly, in a way that was never pushy. I know people would've told her she was being too soft on me.

At family funerals and gatherings, I was always embarrassed when relatives used to ask what I was doing. I don't hold it against them, but it made me feel lousy to have it rubbed in my face that the general norm for an adult who's no longer a student is to be working.

But Mom never tried to hide me away or keep me out of sight. She never pressured me. When my brother comes back, I'm sure that won't change. I was an idiot to think he is more important to her than me. I'll go to the airport with her. We'll welcome him back together.

When my first pay came, I handed all of it to Mom, in an envelope, with a small bouquet of flowers. My way of saying: *Sorry, Mom, and thanks. You must have been worried, but you never showed it.*

But Mom wouldn't accept the envelope. She just pushed it back at me without opening it, then stuck her face into the flowers and cried.

~

When my temporary position came to an end, I was able to stay on, still working part-time. Staff appointments for the new fiscal year had already been made, but Mr. Furuta made a new position for one more person.

"We had a few people apply for it, Hiroya," he tells me, "but I've seen how you work and I want you to stay on."

And that's how I discovered another way to find a job. Filling out CVs, sending them off, getting interviewed and waiting to be chosen, is not the only way to go about it. You can do it like this, too. Just get on with the task in front of you and people will see what you can do.

I have a one-year contract to work four days a week at a rate of 1,100 yen per hour. I can work here and keep drawing, while I take my time to continue the search for my own path.

~

In April, Mrs. Muroi comes to pay us a visit at the Community House with her daughter and grandchild. After thanking me, she tells me in that rapid-fire way of hers that people are saying good things about me. Her daughter is standing behind her as she speaks, holding the baby. The baby stares at me. His neck is still wobbly, and on top of his head he has a single curl of hair, just like Monger.

"Cute, isn't he," says Mrs. Muroi. "This baby has more power over me than any other creature in my life right now."

As she's leaving, Mrs. Muroi says, "By the way I gave a box of Honeydome cookies to Sayuri. Make sure you have some too, Hiroya."

"Thank you. Ms. Komachi really likes those cookies, doesn't she."

Mrs. Muroi gives me a knowing look and snickers. "That's how she met her husband. When they both reached for the same box of Honeydome cookies from a shop shelf and bumped against each other. Apparently he gave her that white flower hairpin she always wears when he proposed, in place of a ring."

This seems incredible at first, but then I smile. It's an awesome story. Everybody should have their own story.

～

In my break I go to the library. Nozomi is in the stacks reshelving, but calls out when she notices me: "The book you reserved is back."

She's referring to a world encyclopedia of deep-sea

fish. I need it to prepare my entry for an art magazine contest. My ambition now is to master a niche corner for illustrations of grotesque but humorous and lovable creatures.

As I'm sitting at the reading table with the encyclopedia open in front of me, I hear the *tatatatatata* rattle of Ms. Komachi pounding the keyboard. I have a partially obscured view of a man behind the partition wearing a waist pouch, no doubt being given a recommendation.

"Yep, you're Kenshiro all right," I automatically mutter to myself. But Ms. Komachi's technique has taught me an extremely simple truth. In the long, long history of evolution, without doubt, I am living now, in the present.

5

Masao, 65, retired

The last day of September, when I turned sixty-five, was also my last day working for the company. I did not have any outstanding achievements to show for my forty-two years there, but nor was my record blemished in any way. I had risen to the position of manager and my diligence was duly recognized. On the day I left, I was presented with a bouquet of flowers and departed to applause and a chorus of good wishes:

Thank you for your hard work.

Thanks for everything.

Take care.

I felt relief, mingled with wistfulness and a sense of accomplishment. Every day for forty-two years I had boarded a train at a set time, traveling to the same office to sit in my designated seat and do the work I was given. In the course of my career, I encountered many challenges that I dealt with the best I could. The day the curtain came down on that life, I took one last good long look at the office building, bowed deeply and turned my back on it.

~

And then, well…? What am I going to do now?

~

The cherry blossom season is nearly over. Perhaps I should go and see the blossoms again tomorrow. On second thoughts, perhaps not. I've already seen plenty. Usually, I would rush out at the weekend in early April to catch the blossoms before they fell, but this year has been different. I have had the leisure to follow their progress from bud through to full bloom. I was able to go and view them whenever the fancy took me, at any time of day or night. When my daughter, Chie, was young I was always too busy to take weekends off, and often we didn't get to see the blossoms together. Now that I finally have the time, however, Chie is not at home anymore. She lives on her own nowadays, but even if she were still at home, I doubt if she would accompany her father to view the blossoms.

In the six months since my retirement, I have learned three things. One is that sixty-five is not as old as I thought. This came as a surprise—I am not at all like the old man I used to imagine that I would become. Of course, I haven't been young for quite some time now, but I certainly don't feel old yet. More like middle-aged.

The second thing is that I have a worrying lack of hobbies. I do have a number of small pleasures. Things I look forward to, such as my evening beer, or watching the latest epic historical drama on Sunday evenings. But these are part of my everyday life and not the same thing as a hobby. I don't make anything and I don't have any kind of all-absorbing interest that I can talk about with passion.

The third thing I have learned... Sigh. The third thing is that now that I no longer work for a company I am no longer acknowledged by society at large.

Talking to people had been part of my job as I was in the sales department for many years. Which is why I may have been under the mistaken impression that I had a wide personal network. It was a shock when New Year came after I retired, and I received none of the usual cards or end-of-year gifts. I was shaken to realize that all my relationships had been business ones, and that I had no real friends after all, not even somebody to drink tea with. Over the last six months all trace of my existence at the company will have faded away. Despite my forty-two years there.

~

I am sitting idly in front of the television when Yoriko arrives home from work. She looks around the room, makes a clucking sound, then stalks over to the balcony entrance.

"Really, Masao. Didn't I ask you to bring the laundry in?"

Damn. I forgot the laundry. But Yoriko isn't really angry—I can tell.

"Dopey head," she says, as if scolding a child. She opens the sliding glass door to the balcony and puts on outdoor slippers to go and bring in the washing.

"Sorry," I say as she hands me the laundry through the door and I carry it inside. The dry clothes smell of sunshine.

I've never done housework and still find it hard to get used to. If Yoriko asks me to do something for her, it just seems to slip from my mind. But if I keep on loafing about at home like this, both my body and brain will run to seed and I'll end up a senile old man. Now might be the only time Yoriko laughs at my forgetfulness. She is very forgiving, but that might only be a sign she thinks that anger is futile, because she has already given up on me.

With grim determination, I proceed to take the laundry off the pegs. But then I am not sure how to fold the socks and underwear, so I pick out the towels and do these.

"Oh, Masao, by the way," Yoriko says, "I brought you this." She hands me a flyer from her bag. The heading in large letters at the top reads "Go Class."

"Remember I told you about Mr. Yakita, one of my students? He started teaching a Go class at the Community House in April and I thought you might be interested."

"Mr Yakita? The old man who was making a web page about wildflowers?"

"Yes, that's the one. His Go class fee is monthly, but since April is half over he offered to let you pay only half."

Yoriko used to be a systems engineer at an IT company until she was forty. She works freelance now and is registered with an association through which she receives requests to teach computer classes and courses. That's how she came to be at this place where she's teaching now, the Community House. She goes there every Wednesday. I don't know much about computers myself, but I do know that having IT skills is important these days. And in Yoriko's field of work, there is also no retirement age.

"The Community House is only ten minutes' walk. You know the place, next to Hatori Elementary. They're joined together."

"Go, you say... I've never tried it."

"All the better. Learning from scratch will be an interesting exercise for you," she replies from the kitchen, where she is now tying an apron around her waist.

At fifty-six, Yoriko is nine years younger than I am. My young bride, people used to call her when we got married. Although nobody calls her that anymore, she still seems to think of herself as a young wife. And she is in fact youthful and active. She also still works. Women in their fifties nowadays seem to shine at their work with a confidence that is quite dazzling.

So, Yoriko thinks I should play Go… I examine the flyer and picture how that might seem: *Yes, my hobby is Go…* It's nothing out of the ordinary, but it might not be a bad thing to try out. At the very least, it will give my brain some exercise.

The class is on Monday mornings at eleven. I consult our joint calendar, and of course there is nothing written down for me at this time. All the entries on it are Yoriko's.

∼

When Monday morning comes, I set out for the Community House. I know where Hatori Elementary School is, and find it easily enough, but the front gate is firmly locked. I press the intercom button at the gate and a woman answers.

"Hello, I'm here for the Go class," I tell her.

"Excuse me?"

"The Go class, at the Community House."

"Aha, I see."

The woman proceeds to tell me that there is a separate entrance for the Community House, and I should follow the fence around to the signboard that will indicate the way. Slightly disgruntled that the Community House is not in fact joined to the school, as I had been led to believe, I follow the fence as instructed, as far as a signboard that informs me: "Community House this way." Eventually I reach a white building at the end of a narrow street, which is separated from the schoolyard by a fence. Inside the front entrance there is a reception desk immediately to the right. In an office area behind this desk, a young man in a green shirt with a thick mop of hair is working at a computer. He comes out when he notices me.

"Fill in this form, please," he says, pointing to a list on the counter with spaces to fill in for name, purpose of visit and time of arrival and departure.

"I had trouble finding this place," I tell him. "My wife said it was joined to the elementary school, so I assumed they were in the same grounds."

The man laughs. "This place used to be connected to the elementary school but access is blocked now for security reasons."

"You don't say."

"Yes, it's a real shame because the original purpose of the Community House was to promote interaction between the children and local residents. But there've been too many nasty incidents, I suppose. The children's safety and security come first, and now even the school front gate is kept locked. Many students leave Hatori Elementary without ever once coming in here."

I make the appropriate noises as he speaks, while I fill in my name and other details.

Masao Gonno. Nobody says my name out loud much these days. The last time was at the dentist's, a month ago.

I find the Go class in the Japanese-style room. Removing my shoes, I step up on to the tatami mat. Already there are people engaged in playing each other over the Go boards. An old man with a square jaw sitting alone at the back of the room calls out to me.

"Mr. Gonno? Welcome to the class. Your wife has told me about you."

"Thank you for allowing me to participate."

"Not at all. You're welcome."

It feels strange to exchange such banal social pleasantries again. I haven't done this in quite a while.

Yoriko had told me that Mr. Yakita is seventy-five, but he looks hale and hearty, and his skin glows. He indicates for me to sit and places a Go board between us. Then he commences to explain the rules, starting from the very beginning. He tells me how to place the stones, where to place them, the order in which to place them, and how to decide who makes the first move. I listen attentively, my eyes fastened on the board, and nod at everything.

Then, quite abruptly, he says, "Your wife is wonderful."

Startled, I look up to see him stroking his chin thoughtfully.

"I envy you. Mrs. Gonno is very intelligent and quick-witted, also good at her work. I'm done with marriage myself."

From this I gather he is divorced and single. Nonplussed, I make an ambiguous reply and try to focus on the Go stones again. This, however, has the effect of prompting Mr. Yakita to launch into a monologue.

"You see a lot of late-life divorce these days. Arguments between husband and wife can be all right if one goes out to work every day. You might have a spat in the morning, but by the time you get home at night, things have more or less blown over. But if you're at home all the time, and in each other's pockets all day, well, there's no opportunity to step back and let things reset. We'd been together so many years, I didn't think much about it. Every Jack has his Jill. You know how it is."

"I beg your pardon?"

"What you have to understand about women is that

they can reach a certain point when all of a sudden every little thing that's ever irritated them becomes too much to bear anymore, just like that. Toward the end, even my taste in socks was too much for her. "What on earth are you wearing?" she'd say."

This teacher obviously likes to talk. Maybe hearing about his private life is an initiation ceremony for joining this class. I can't help stealing a look at his socks and observing that they have a fish-scale-like pattern. But if that's the reason his wife left, then I feel sorry for him. I smile tightly as Mr. Yakita continues his story.

"It was a bolt from the blue when she presented me with the divorce papers, I can tell you. But I've no shortage of things to keep me busy. I've been playing Go since I was a teenager, and I garden and look for wildflowers. So I thought, well why not, maybe we can both go back to being single again, and enjoy life on our own. If anything, it was all for the best, I think."

Is this the secret, then? If you throw yourself into doing the things you like, it's possible to live a happy, healthy life as he does, even if one is old, retired, divorced and living alone. Mr. Yakita also has status as a Go teacher, and there is bound to be some Go association he belongs to, not to mention all the contacts from his interest in plants. That website he learned to make in Yoriko's class must attract people.

"My wife started changing her attitude toward me about six months after I retired," he says, lowering his voice, as if to emphasize that this is more important than the rules of Go. "Time for you to be on your guard, start paying attention."

~

Go turns out to be a lot more difficult than I thought. I was not allowed to take notes while listening to Mr. Yakita's verbal instructions, and nothing seemed to stick in my head. At the end of the lesson I was ready to throw in the towel, but having paid for two lessons in advance, I don't want to waste my money by not coming again.

While putting on my shoes to leave, the same young man in the green shirt from reception walks past me and disappears through a door at the end of the corridor with a sign above it that says "Library."

I hadn't realized that this place has a library. Perhaps it has books on Go. I follow in the young man's tracks and enter through the same doorway to investigate. The library is a cosy space with tightly packed shelves lining the walls. The young man is chatting with a girl in a navy-blue apron, but otherwise there is nobody else in here. I start to wander around, searching for Go books, when the girl in the apron walks by holding several books in her arms. The name tag on her chest reads "Nozomi Morinaga."

"Excuse me, could you tell me where I can find books about Go, please?"

Nozomi Morinaga bestows on me a smile as radiant as a sunflower. "Over there," she says pointing with one hand to a shelf on the opposite side of the room. "Please follow me."

The shelf labeled "Entertainment" has many books about Go and shogi—far more than I expected.

"We have a large selection," Nozomi says, as her gaze travels over the shelf. "But choosing can be difficult because, in the beginning, you don't know what you don't know."

She seems to be a sensitive young woman, attuned to the feelings of library patrons. I imagine she would be a dependable member of staff.

"I've never played Go myself, but I'm sure the librarian could help with selecting some suitable texts for you. She's over there."

I did not think the situation warranted asking a librarian for advice, but if Nozomi thought it was a good idea, then I was willing to try.

Making my way to the back of the room, I see a sign hanging from the ceiling that says "Reference." The screen partitioning off this area also functions as a bulletin board. However, when I make my way to the other side, my feet stop dead at the sight of a very large woman. Her white button-up shirt is so tight the buttons look in danger of popping off, and her extremely pale skin reminds me of a white glutinous rice cake in a shrine at New Year. A white floral hairpin pierces the small bun of hair perched on the very top of her head.

She is busy doing something with her hands, which continue to move without stopping while she keeps looking down, so I don't think she can be aware of me. When I look closer, I see she is poking a needle into something resembling a lump of fur. I sense anger in her expression, and she seems unapproachable.

I don't really need to go to the trouble of asking anybody for advice. I can find a book for myself, I decide. Then, at that moment, a familiar shade of orange catches my eye. The lid of the box that is facedown near the librarian's hands has a hexagonal border design based on a beehive, with white acacia flowers in the center. I would know that design anywhere. It's a Honeydome cookie box, from Kuremiyado, the company where I worked for so many years. I notice it contains needles and scissors, though, not cookies. She must be using the empty box for her sewing tools. I lean further forward for a better look.

Abruptly, the librarian looks up. "What are you looking for?" she says, in a calm, dignified voice. I feel it resonating deep down inside me.

What am I looking for? What am *I looking for?*
A new way to live from now on, perhaps?

The librarian stares at me. Now that my eyes meet hers, I understand that the expression I had taken for anger at first is not that at all. Rather, it is more like the profound compassion of a Goddess of Mercy.

"I would like a book about Go. I tried it for the first time today and it soon started to become quite complicated."

The name tag on the librarian's chest reads "Sayuri Komachi." Ms. Komachi lets her head roll to one side with a crack, then puts the needle and lump of fur away in the box and closes the lid.

"There is a lot more to Go than meets the eye," she replies. "It's not just about taking your opponent's territory. Each game has its own drama that forces you to think about life and death."

"Oh, is it that serious?"

It doesn't sound at all like entertainment. I thought hobbies were supposed to be amusing and fun.

"In that case I'm not sure it's the right kind of thing for me," I say, scratching my head. "Do you like these?" I ask, pointing at the box to change the subject.

Ms. Komachi grunts and swivels her gaze, which now rests on the box.

"They're Kuremiyado Honeydome cookies. I used to work there, actually, up until last year."

Ms. Komachi's eyes snap wide open and she sucks in her breath with a whoosh. With a smile, she begins singing out loud, as if possessed, her unfocused eyes staring into the distance.

How, how, how?
How is it, how are you, how am I, how is it?
How, how, how is your Honeydome?
Kuremiyado Honeydome!

She is singing the jingle from the Honeydome commercial. A song that has not changed in the last thirty years. Ms. Komachi's voice is a falsetto, so thin it is hard to believe that it comes from that large frame. She sings quietly, enough for it not to travel beyond the partition, but on the last syllable of "Honeydome" at the very end, she allows herself to belt out an extended *doooooome* with a joyful, childlike expression.

This comes out of nowhere, taking me utterly by surprise. I experience a warm flush of happiness so intense it makes me feel like crying. When the song is over, Ms. Komachi resumes her normal straight face again.

"There's an English verse too, isn't there?"

"Yes, that's right."

The last verse of the jingle is in English. A nod to the wish for these cookies to be enjoyed by people of all ages and nationalities.

Ms. Komachi bows her head respectfully to me. "Thank you for these wonderful cookies."

I smile wryly. "It's not as though I made them myself."

That's the nub of it. I didn't even make these sweets and yet I have spent decades recommending them to others as my own, simply because I was an employee of Kuremiyado. Even now, it makes me feel happy to hear them praised.

"But I no longer work for Kuremiyado." It hurts to even say this.

Ms. Komachi turns to look at me with an expression so composed that I have the urge to open up my heart to this large, pale woman, who—and this might sound impolite—is somehow not like other ordinary human beings. Behind those eyes I sense a large and magnanimous heart, open and accepting of everything. I realize how badly I have been longing for someone to listen to me.

"It has been my experience that, for a company man like myself, retiring from work is the same as retiring from society. When I was working, I occasionally thought it would be nice to take some time off, but now that I actually do have time, I don't know what to do with it. The remainder of my life feels meaningless."

"What do you mean by "the remainder"?" Ms. Komachi replies, without batting an eyelid.

I ask myself the same thing. What *do* I mean by "the remainder"?

"The leftover part, I suppose. What remains," I say.

She rolls her head in the opposite direction. "Let's say you ate ten Honeydome cookies from a box of twelve."

"I beg your pardon?"

"Would the last two be 'remainders'?"

I cannot answer straight away. This question, I suspect, touches on the heart of the matter, but as I don't feel capable of voicing my answer, I stay mum.

Ms. Komachi straightens her back and turns to face the computer. She places both hands on the keyboard, as if she is about to start playing the piano, and then proceeds to attack the keys at an astounding speed with a *zu-da-da-da-da-daaa*. It's miraculous the way her plump fingers move so swiftly. I am still gaping with my mouth half open when she gives one final crash on the keys. Next moment the printer begins printing and churns out a single-sheet document.

When she hands it to me, I see it is a table, with a list of book titles, with author names and shelf numbers.

The Basics of Go: Defend and Attack, Starting Go from Scratch, Mastering Go for Beginners. And lastly, this title,

Genge and Frogs, with the words "Junior Poetry Series" next to it in brackets, and the author's name, Shinpei Kusano.

Poetry? Shinpei Kusano was a poet, it's true. But why this?

While I examine the sheet of paper, Ms. Komachi reaches into a wooden cabinet under the counter. She opens the bottom drawer, digs through the contents and takes something out.

"Here, this is for you," she says holding out her hand, bunched into a fist. I open my own hand and Ms. Komachi drops a red fluffy ball into it. The shape is squarish and it has two small, scissor-like projections.

"Is this a crab?"

"It's a bonus gift."

"A bonus gift?"

"Yes, a bonus to go with the books."

"Aha," I say, although I don't really understand. I asked about Go but I get frogs and crabs... I look at my crab again. Its legs are quite realistic.

"This is called felting," Ms. Komachi tells me. "You can make things in any shape or size. There is no limit to what you can do with it."

She does felting? Now that makes me envious. I wouldn't mind a hobby like this. Just one hobby would be enough.

"This kind of thing is also called work—handiwork," she says in a meaningful tone.

"I beg your pardon?" I ask.

In response, she opens the lid of the Honeydome box, and resumes her handiwork, looking down as she pokes at what I can now see is a ball of wool. It feels like a barrier has been put in place, with the object of keeping people at bay. Sensing that any further discussion would be an imposition, I put the crab in my waist pouch and head for the stacks, taking the document with me.

~

After dinner that evening, taking all the books I borrowed as recommended by Ms. Komachi, I retire to the spare room. It used to be Chie's bedroom, but ever since she moved out, we have used it as a combined storage and multipurpose room.

I purchased this three-bedroom condominium at the age of thirty-five when it was brand-new. Now it is falling into disrepair and showing its age. But since we hardly have visitors anymore, anything that doesn't inconvenience us is left as it is. There are stains on the walls, holes in the paper sliding doors, and squeaky hinges. We turned the Japanese-style tatami room into our bedroom and use the other one as a computer room. That is Yoriko's domain. I hesitate even to set foot inside.

I seat myself at Chie's old study desk and place the

books on it. First, I flip through the Go textbooks. Although these are what I requested, I have to say they don't really excite me. I don't anticipate discovering any life-or-death dramas in them. The only book that stirs any kind of feeling in me is *Genge and Frogs*, the one I borrowed almost by mistake. The cover is a charming illustration of a country scene featuring three frogs with happy relaxed faces. A stream cuts through the middle, flanked on both sides by pink, cherry blossom-like balls. It's a bright cheerful crayon picture—exactly the kind of thing that would tempt a child to pick it up.

I turn the pages until I come to an introduction entitled "Relating to Poetry." The author is not Shinpei Kusano, but the editor, Takashi Sawa. As the word "Junior" in the title suggests, the book is one of a series for children, written in suitably simple language, yet Takashi Sawa still manages to convey, loud and clear, his passion for Kusano Shinpei and his poetry.

He recommends transcribing any poem that you happen to like into a notebook. It can be the whole poem or just a section. In this way, you can create your own anthology.

When you are in contact with the poet's soul and their attitude to life, your response to their poetry becomes even more powerful. You can, in a sense, even enter into life of that poet and feel moved in the same way.

I wondered about that. It seems rather an exaggeration to say we could enter into the life of the poet. Then I read the line "And if you too feel the urge to write poetry yourself, by all means please do so," which makes me laugh out loud. Definitely not. But I could transcribe verse. Simply writing down part of a poem sounds easy enough, and the word "anthology" has a nice ring to it—it sounds clever. It would be easier than learning Go, I expect, yet still count as an intellectual activity. I like the sound of this.

But I need a notebook. I rummage through the desk drawer and fish out an old ruled college notebook. The first two pages have some short sentences in English, and the alphabet, in my handwriting.

I'd forgotten this. About twenty years ago, I attempted to study English through a course on the radio. Even I had had a modicum of ambition to learn. I have the feeling I thought it might be useful for work, or maybe I just wanted a new interest. But I remember thinking that, after forty, it was too late to learn anything and soon gave up. If I'd kept it up and studied one page a day, I might be fluent by now.

Well, it will never be filled with English. I tear out

the pages and turn it into a fresh notebook. Then I turn it on its side to write vertically, Japanese-style. After reading three poems in *Genge and Frogs*, I copy down the first one, "Song of Spring," with a marker pen that I find in the pen stand.

Hoh, it's so bright.
Hoh, happy day,

Smooth water.
Gentle wind.
Ke-ru-run, ku-ku.
Ah, wonderful smells.

There's more, but I put the pen down here. The line "*Ke-ru-run, ku-ku*" is repeated four times in all, and I guess it is the call of a frog. It has a nice rhythm, and cleverly matches the beat of the poem.

Time goes by as I become absorbed in reading all the poems. I had assumed the tone of the rest would be as light and bright as 'Song of Spring," but some are wistful and some are dark. There is quite a variety.

Then I come across one called "*Kajika.*" It's a strange poem.

Ki-ki-ki-ki-ki-ki-ki-ki
Kiiru-kiiru-kiiru-kiiru-kiiru

From the very first line it has a striking sound. The more I transcribe, the more its mystery deepens. What makes this sound? Isn't a *kajika* a type of fish? Or maybe it's a deer. There is no explanation and I can't work it out. I can't even picture what the phrases "night caught in the borderline" or 'flicker of gills" might be describing.

I get as far as copying "*Ki-ki-ki-ki-ki-ki-ki-ki*," then stop. Understanding poetry is not as easy as it seems. Could it be even more challenging than learning the rules of Go? I close the notebook.

~

The next afternoon, Yoriko and I go on an outing to a big store called Eden, a place I'm not too familiar with. But Yoriko recently learned that a student from her computer class works in the womenswear department there and she wants to go shopping. Yoriko is what you might call a "driver on paper." She nominally has her driving license but never actually drives, and since Eden is too far to go on foot, she has asked me to take her there today. I have no reason not to.

On our way to the car park in our building, she spies the building superintendent, Mr. Ebigawa, and calls out to him. He is in early old age, I guess, and replaced the previous superintendent at the beginning of the year. He is in the middle of pulling weeds from the shrubbery and turns to look at us.

Yoriko bows with a smile. "Thank you for your help the other day. I cleaned my bicycle as you suggested and the brakes work much better now."

Last week when she ran into Mr. Ebigawa at the bicycle parking area, he gave her some advice on how use detergent to clean a part called the brake shoe to improve the effectiveness of her brakes.

"You're welcome. I'm glad it did the trick. I used to have a bicycle shop a long time ago."

He gives a mellow smile and goes back to pulling weeds. Mr. Ebigawa is not surly, but he is by no means a man of many words.

"Mr. Ebigawa looks like a completely different person whenever I bump into him away from here," Yoriko says once we are out of earshot. "When he's not in his work clothes, he always wears a smart knitted cap. Maybe that's why."

"A different person? In what way?"

"It's hard to say... He looks like an ascetic sage who lives in the mountains. Someone who is not part of the mundane world. But when he's in his superintendent's uniform and sitting in the office, he looks just like any ordinary person."

When we arrive at Eden, I park the car and Yoriko leads me straight to the womenswear department upstairs.

"Tomoka."

The sales assistant's face breaks into a big smile. "Mrs. Gonno! You really came. Welcome."

"Yes, I made it. This is my husband, Masao."

Tomoka gives me a beautiful bow with both hands placed precisely together in front of her. "It's my pleasure to meet you. I am indebted to your wife."

"Not at all, the pleasure is mine."

Like Mr. Ebigawa, Tomoka is another of Yoriko's acquaintances. Sometimes it feels as if she is my only link to society now. Yoriko begins to rummage through the clothes, while I twiddle my thumbs gazing around at all the blouses and skirts there are in the store.

I estimate Tomoka to be in her early twenties. She seems to be an energetic and efficient young lady. She certainly gives the impression of being cheerful and enthusiastic about her work.

"May I try this on?" Yoriko holds up a dress.

"Yes, of course," Tomoka replies, opening the curtain to the fitting room.

When the two of us are on our own, Tomoka makes conversation with me. "How lovely that you go shopping as a couple. You must get along well."

"I probably get in her way now that I'm home all the

time. I can't even do the housework. I wish I could at least cook, but it's not easy."

Tomoka appears to think this over for a few moments. Then, with a bright smile, she says, "Why don't you try making rice balls?"

"Rice balls? Do you think my wife would like that?"

"I'm sure she'd love it. Rice balls made by men taste really good. Maybe it's because they have strong hands that can firmly shape the rice. In any case, I'm sure Mrs. Gonno would be thrilled if you made her some."

"Thrilled, do you think so?" I say with a smile. "Did your boyfriend happen to make rice balls for you, perhaps?"

Tomoka's cheeks turn bright red, but she does not deny it.

～

Yoriko purchases a dress and a cat print T-shirt, then suggests we go to the food hall to buy something for dinner. We go to the fish section to choose sashimi, and there, alongside the glass cases filled with fish and shellfish, I spy a small stand. A movement inside it catches my eye and I take a closer look. The plastic container is full of live river crabs, fifty or sixty of them, all massed together in a small amount of water. Recalling the crab that Ms. Komachi had given me, I gaze at the creatures awhile to examine them. Some wave the small scissor claws attached to their flat bodies as if sending out signals.

Then I raise my eyes to a signboard made from Styrofoam that is pinned above the box, and experience a sudden jolt.

Below the words "river crabs" written prominently in red is a line in smaller black lettering that says, "For deep-frying! For pets!"

For pets...?

It is natural in the food section to expect that crabs would be sold for consumption, but when suddenly presented with the option of keeping them as a pet, instead, I don't know what to think.

Be eaten or be loved.

A lump forms in my throat at the thought of the utterly different fates awaiting these crabs huddled together in the plastic box.

When I worked for the company, what kind of crab was I, I wonder. While still inside the box I was raised to be a manager, but ultimately wasn't my fate to be eaten up by the organization?

At this point Yoriko, who has been inspecting sashimi all the while, suddenly turns to ask, "Shall we have horse mackerel or saury? Oh, look, there are crabs. What about those?" She examines them with interest.

"No." I can barely squeeze the word out. "No, they're still alive. We can't eat them."

"Would you like some to keep as pets?" she jokes.

How would that work? I think it through. Would the crabs be happy spending the rest of their lives in a boring, narrow case? Perhaps they would actually prefer to be part of the maelstrom in the food chain? Or is it simply my human ego that dictates this way of thinking?

I remain silent when Yoriko's messaging app pings.

"Ah, it's Chie."

Yoriko skilfully manipulates the controls of her smartphone and has a chirpy exchange with Chie.

"The book I ordered has arrived," she reports to me after hanging up. "Why don't we forget about buying supper here and stop by Chie's shop instead? If she's on the early shift, she'll finish at four and we could all go out for dinner together."

This suggestion cheers me slightly. Before we leave, I take another peep at the river crabs and say a prayer for their happiness. Whatever that may be.

~

Chie, our daughter and only child, works for a chain store called Meishin Books at a branch near the station. She is twenty-seven years old and single. After graduating from college, she joined the company as a contract employee and left home at the same time. She lives on her own in an apartment.

Yoriko visits the bookshop quite frequently for one reason or another, but I rarely do. I feel uncomfortable with the idea of a parent sniffing around their child's place of work.

When we arrive, Chie is out on the shop floor attending to a customer. Yoriko and I watch from a distance as the elderly woman quizzes Chie, whose face wears an expression we don't see at home—a gentle open smile that nevertheless comes across as sharp and focused.

The old woman gives a satisfied nod then bows and takes her book over to the till. While seeing off the customer, Chie catches sight of us. She is wearing a white-collared shirt and dark-green work apron. There is no uniform, apart from these dress requirements. With her short, neat haircut, the outfit suits her.

"I made this display," she says when we go over to her.

The point-of-purchase display consists of a postcard-sized card placed beside a row of copies of the same book, arranged face out. The card shows the book title and a concise, lively summary of the contents. When Yoriko praises her work, Chie looks proud.

"These POP displays are so important, you know. They can really make a difference to sales."

After the incident with the river crabs, I can certainly believe it. If it hadn't been for that sign, I never would have given a second thought to the fate of those crabs.

"What time do you finish?" Yoriko asks. "If it's early, how about going out for dinner with us?"

Chie shakes her head. "I'm on the late shift today. Besides, I have to help set up for an event."

Working in a bookshop is physically demanding. Besides standing up all day, the staff must handle stock, which can be heavy, and deal with all manner of tasks and inquiries from customers. I had heard through Yoriko that one of Chie's colleagues had been hospitalized due to a work-related back injury. I worry about her.

"Be careful, don't injure yourself," I tell her.

"Don't worry. Tomorrow's my day off," Chie reassures me. She looks happy.

Day off. That reminds me of one more thing I learned since retiring: if you don't work, there are no days off. Never again will I enjoy the anticipation of freedom and feeling of release at the thought of taking time off work.

Chie turns to Yoriko. "You came to get the book, right?"

"Yes. And I want to pick up some magazines. Wait here while I get them."

Yoriko strides over to the magazine section and I wonder if I should buy something too, but there's nothing I

270

can think of that I want. On the spur of the moment I
say to Chie, "Whereabouts are the poetry books?"

Her eyes grow wide. "Poetry books? Who, for example?"

"Shinpei Kusano."

Chie's face lights up. "I like his poetry, too. It was
in our elementary school textbook. There was one that
went '*Ke-ru-run ku-ku*.'"

"That would be 'Song of Spring.'"

"Yes, it is. Not bad, Dad."

Feeling pleased with myself, I follow Chie over to the
children's section, where I find a copy of *Genge and Frog*s.
I turn the pages until I come to "*Kajika.*"

"Do you know what the title of this one means?
What's a *kajika*?"

"I'm pretty sure it's a type of frog. A singing frog."

Aha, mystery solved. It was a frog after all.

"The teacher taught us some other poems by Shinpei
Kusano. That's how I know that the title of the book,
Genge, means 'lotus root.'"

"So that's what it means. I have to say his poems sometimes confuse me."

"With poetry you don't have to worry too much about
the finer nuances of meaning. Just enjoy the feel or sound
of a poem as you read it. Imagine it however you like."

Yoriko arrives back and I return the book to the shelf.

"This looks great," she says, holding up the thick magazine in her hands. "I want the bonus gift bag that comes with it."

This bonus gift, packed between the pages, is the reason the magazine is so thick. I remember my own bonus gift in my waist pouch and open it to look. The red crab peeks out from inside.

"Oh, it's a crab!" Chie exclaims. For some reason her cheeks flush.

"Would you like it?"

She takes it in her hand, looking pleased. My heart melts at the sight. If such things can make her happy, then she is indeed still a child.

~

In the end Yoriko and I go out for dinner by ourselves. When we arrive home, I go to the spare room and open up *Genge and Frogs* again. Now I know that a *kajika* is a type of frog, the poem is rather charming. A frog croaking makes complete sense. But the other lines, the ones that aren't the sound of a frog croaking with joy at the return of spring, seem deeply profound.

I still don't fully understand what "night caught in the borderline" or "flicker of gills" means, but in the darkness of night an image of dripping water unfolds in my mind. Like something...the universe perhaps...shining as it flaps open and shut...with a receding echo of the strange sad cry of frogs in the background.

Oh, I did it. That was fun. If this is what "poetry appreciation" is all about, I quite enjoy it. Maybe I do have a smattering of talent in that direction.

I continue browsing in a leisurely way until another poem catches my eye. The title is "Window" and for this collection it is unusually long.

Waves draw close.
Waves pull back.
Waves lick at old stone walls.
In this sunless cove
Waves draw close.
Waves pull back.
Wooden clogs, scraps of straw,
Streaks of oil.

Hmm, clogs, straw and oil... So this scene is describing the man-made debris caused by human beings washing up in a sunless cove. And the lines "Waves draw close. / Waves pull back" are repeated numerous times throughout the poem... Aha—I see what's happening. The poem itself builds an image of the movement of waves. Waves traveling from distant open seas reach the cove, and draw close and then pull back. They come and they go. Evoking an image of vast oceans. The waves draw close. The waves pull back.

And yet… I still don't completely understand. Why is this poem called "Window"? It only describes waves, so why is it "Window" and not "Waves"?

But there is more to the poem. In the second half, which also has descriptions of waves, words like *love*, *hatred* and *corruption* appear. I read each line carefully, through to the end. Then I copy the entire three-page poem into my notebook and read it again, and again.

~

When Monday comes, I don't feel like attending the Go class again, but balk at wasting money. Today will be the last time, I decide. While getting ready to go out, I remember Yoriko's comment about Mr. Ebigawa's stylish caps. Perhaps I should try and be stylish, too. I wish I could ask Yoriko where the hats are kept, but she has gone out. Searching through the closet, I find, stuffed in a corner, a black cap that I had received as a freebie some years ago. This will do. I pull it on my head and depart.

When I reach Hatori Elementary School, the sound of children's cheerful voices echoes from the schoolyard as I pass by the main gate and walk along the fence. I

stop to look over it into the yard. The children are probably in third or fourth grade, and appear to be having
a sports class. My heart warms at the sight of them all
doing warm-up exercises in their short-sleeved shirts
and shorts. What a charming sight. Chie used to be that
young once, too.

Whenever I went on school-observation days, she
would look around eagerly and mouth the word *Daddy*
silently when she caught sight of me. It used to make
me happy. Ah, time goes by so fast, children don't stay
little for very long.

At that moment I become aware I am being watched,
and turn my head to see a young policeman observing
me sharply. I look away and go to walk off, but he calls
out, "Excuse me."

He is making me nervous, though I have done nothing wrong. Pretending not to hear, I walk faster.

"Wait! Stop!"

His loud voice startles me so much I tremble. I have
never been spoken to by a young man in such a manner
before. I stop and stand stiffly in my tracks. The policeman approaches and says sternly, "You were trying to
run away, weren't you, Grandpa."

Grandpa...! This completely knocks the wind out of
my sails. Am I already an old man in the eyes of others?
The policeman fixes me with a steely gaze.

"I'd like you to answer a few questions. What's your name?"

Struggling to pull myself together, I manage to answer, "Gonno. Masao Gonno."

"Occupation?"

I say nothing. What can I say? I have no occupation. I am unemployed. That is the answer I am obliged to give, and my head droops dejectedly at the thought.

"Show me your ID," the policeman demands.

"Show me your ID…?" I repeat, putting my hand inside my waist pouch. A sinking feeling comes over me. The driver's license and health card that I usually carry are not in there. Today I had left home with only a coin purse, since I was not going far.

The policeman sees my stunned expression and asks, "What's wrong?" He comes a step closer.

~

In the end, Yoriko came and got me after I called her on my smartphone. Thank goodness she was home by then. I was immediately let go once she had arrived with our driving licenses, and spoken capably to the policeman.

After that I was in no mood for Go anymore. Besides, the class was almost over, so we set off walking for home.

"That policeman was rude, but you weren't any help," Yoriko chides me. "Why were you so afraid?"

"Because I... It was a shock to be treated like a criminal all of a sudden. All I was doing was watching the children, and thinking how cute they were."

"Oh, really." Yoriko frowns. "Think about that for a moment. If a man, dressed like that, is standing around in the middle of the day grinning at children, he's bound to attract suspicion. Children are the target of all sorts of crimes nowadays."

"What do you mean, 'dressed like that'? My attire is perfectly normal. Not to mention my stylish cap."

Yoriko points at my head. "That cap, to begin with, is pulled down too far over your eyes and makes you look extremely suspicious."

"This? Surely not!"

"And that tatty old polo shirt and sweatshirt are hardly respectable for going out in. It's exactly what you wear at home." Lowering her voice, she adds, "I don't know why you have to wear your work shoes with a sweatshirt anyway."

Because these leather shoes that I used to wear for work are worn in and comfortable, far more than a brand-new pair of sneakers, I want to tell her. And if I'm going in and out of a tatami room where the Go class is held, they are much easier to put on and off. Does clothing determine if a person looks suspicious? Would I have attracted attention today if I had been wearing a suit?

In trepidation I ask Yoriko this. "Are leather shoes with a sweatshirt so terrible?"

"You would need a very advanced fashion sense to be able to pull that off," she says dryly. It suddenly dawns on me that Yoriko does not like my taste in clothes. I remember the numerous occasions when I put out a shirt in readiness to wear, and somehow another one mysteriously appeared in its place, and the times Yoriko has asked me in a roundabout way if I really like my waist pouch. She has never said outright that I have bad taste, but what if she is just barely managing to tolerate it. Like Mr. Yakita's ex-wife. The word "divorce" suddenly flashes through my mind.

"In any case, the worst thing you can do is run away from a policeman."

"I didn't run away. He just thought I did." I remember him calling me Grandpa and start to feel depressed again. Perhaps it is not a good idea to tell Yoriko about that. I look down at my leather shoes in dejection.

≈

Several days after this incident, a cardboard box full of pomelos arrives, as a gift from Yoriko's relative who has orchards in Ehime Prefecture.

"Oh, these are lovely. Let's give Mr. Ebigawa some in return for his help with the bicycle." She picks out several nice pomelos and puts them in a plastic bag. "Here, you take them to him."

"What?"

"You use the bicycle, too, don't you, Masao?"

"Well, I suppose I do."

And you have the time. Which Yoriko does not say but which I can hear her thinking.

I pick up the bag and head for the superintendent's office, next to the front entrance. The sliding window of the small office is usually kept closed, with the superintendent opening it from the inside as necessary.

Mr Ebigawa is seated diagonally opposite the window, staring blankly at something. He looks up when I call him through the glass and takes the trouble to come and open the door, rather than the window, to speak to me. I hold the plastic bag out to him.

"We received a box of pomelos from a relative in Ehime. Please have these."

"Thank you."

Behind him a row of monitors show images from a security camera. Presumably this is what he had been watching.

"Do you and your wife like sweet bean jelly?" he asks.

"Ah, yes we do."

279

"Somebody gave me some the other day but I don't like red bean paste. You'd be doing me a favor if you took it. Wait a moment."

Was the sweet bean jelly a thank-you gift from somebody else? Mr. Ebigawa must receive all sorts of gifts from residents. What if he doesn't like pomelos?

The superintendent's office is larger than it appears from the outside. From the doorway I can see through to a small sink and storage shelves at the back. It's a splendid office space, with racks full of files, a stack of paperwork on the desk and a whiteboard on the wall. And the large window.

"Window..." I murmur thoughtfully.

Mr Ebigawa looks at me inquiringly. He is holding a paper bag bearing the logo of a Japanese confectionery store.

"Er... I was just wondering what exactly a building superintendent does," I blurt out. "I'm retired now, too much time on my hands. So if the right opportunity came along..."

I'd spoken without thinking, but once the words were past my lips, I realized they were not untrue. I'm healthy, with time to spare, and find it hard to be without employment. There's no reason why I shouldn't look for another job. But having only ever worked at one company, I can't think how one would go about finding another job. That was why I chose to stay on until I was sixty-five instead of retiring at sixty.

"Come in," Mr. Ebigawa says softly, and I enter the room. "As a rule, residents are not allowed in here," he tells me. "So if anyone says anything, please tell them that you were here to ask my advice about improvements to the management committee."

Then he proceeds to tell me about what a building superintendent does. What it involves, the hourly wage and where positions are advertised. It turns out he is a year older than me.

As he speaks, I see people coming and going in both directions on the other side of the window. Residents, visitors and delivery couriers. Children, adults and the elderly. I think of "Window." *Waves draw close. Waves pull back.*

So this is what Mr. Ebigawa sees, watching from his window. Day after day, people coming and going.

"All kinds of people pass by here," I observe.

"Yes. It's strange how a single pane of glass separating the outside from in here can make it seem like two completely different worlds. It's like looking at fish in an aquarium. From the other side, though, this office must look like a small fishbowl." Mr. Ebigawa laughs.

That's very true. An inorganic substance such as glass, despite being transparent, can have the effect of being a solid barrier of sorts. The other day I saw a young couple arguing loudly near the entrance. Seemingly oblivious to whoever might be on the other side of the window. But they stopped when they noticed me. Mr. Ebigawa would have heard everything.

An elderly lady with a bent back walks slowly by. As she passes the office she looks in this direction and gives a quick bow of her head. Following Mr. Ebigawa's lead, I bow mine in return. I've seen her about, but don't know which floor she lives on.

"Good. She's looking well today," Mr. Ebigawa says. "She usually passes by here around the same time each day. She lives on her own, so I keep an eye out for her. I used to be an osteopath and can tell how a person is doing from the way they walk."

"You were an osteopath as well as a bicycle-shop owner?"

Mr. Ebigawa laughs. "I've tried my hand at various jobs. It's my temperament. Once I start thinking about something I want to do, I'm not satisfied until I try it."

"My goodness... It must come in very useful for handling all manner of situations later on."

"Perhaps. But that's not what I think about whenever I begin something new. I do whatever moves me—that's all the reason I need," he replies.

This strikes me as a home truth. Have I ever felt that way about anything?

"I can't tell you how many times I've changed jobs. I was a salaryman for a while too, and went from one company to another. I've been a factory worker in a paper mill, done housecleaning, worked at an insurance company, run a bicycle shop, and a ramen shop. Oh, and I also had an antique shop."

"An antique shop?"

Mr. Ebigawa's face wrinkles into a smile. "I didn't make any money but I enjoyed it. In the end I had to close the shop because I was in debt. But while I was away, seeing about a new job, somebody I'd borrowed money from got it into his head that I'd done a runner. The police did a search. I worked to pay back the money, but until recently my regular customers were still under the impression I was on the run. The police make a lot of noise when they're searching but they don't go around telling people when a case is solved."

I shake my head vigorously in agreement, remembering my own recent run-in with a policeman.

"But the police were only doing their job," Mr. Ebigawa continues. "I'm to blame for not contacting my acquaintances to let them know."

I stop shaking my head. He's right. That young police

officer was just doing his job, protecting the children. As he should—that's a fine thing.

"Is the misunderstanding cleared up now?" I ask.

Mr. Ebigawa smiles. "Yes. One of my regular customers, who is in real estate, has connections with the company that manages this building, so we ran into each other again. I heard from him that a high-school student who often used to come to the shop is getting ready to open his own antique shop. He was a teenager back then so he must be in his mid-thirties now. Though my own shop failed, I'm tickled it inspired someone else. That's a good thing, I think."

Mr Ebigawa looks philosophical. With his leathery skin and deeply etched wrinkles, he looks very much like the ascetic mountain sage that Yoriko had compared him to. Having tried his hand at many different jobs, and had all kinds of experiences over the course of his life, he has achieved the great feat of brightening up someone else's. I would bet my boots he's done that for lots of people, not only this high-school student.

I look down at the ground. "That's marvelous. All I've ever done is work at the same place my whole life and do whatever I was told to. I've never influenced anyone like you have. The minute I left the company, I became superfluous to society."

Mr. Ebigawa smiles kindly. "Society? What *is* society? Is the company the whole of society for you, Mr. Gonno?"

This question stabs me like a needle in the heart, and I put my hand to my breast. Mr. Ebigawa points with his chin in the direction of the window.

"Belonging is an ambiguous state, you know. Take this place, for example. We can both be in the same place, but having that sheet of glass between us makes us feel as if what is happening on the other side is irrelevant, doesn't it. Remove the partition, however, and instantly you become part of the same world. Even though it is all one to begin with."

Mr. Ebigawa looks into my eyes. "This is how I see it, Mr. Gonno. I believe that every kind of contact between people makes them part of society. And that goes beyond the present moment. Things happen as a result of our points of connection, in the past and in the future."

This is a bit above me and I can't quite take in exactly what he's saying. But it's true, as Mr. Ebigawa suggests, that the company had been my whole world. One I can only gaze at now from the other side of a window.

But now, here I am talking with Mr. Ebigawa on this side of a window that I usually walk straight past. And according to the way he sees it, this contact with him here in this place makes me part of society at this moment.

Waves draw close. Waves pull back. Waves lick at old stone walls.

Rough seas are part and parcel of society. From which window did Shinpei Kusano gaze at the sea, I wonder? Why a window, and not the beach? Was it because he knew both faces of the sea, its beauty and ferocity? Is that why he wanted to look at that world from the other side of the glass, apart, as a spectator?

Of course this is all is just my conjecture. But for a brief time, I feel as if I have entered into his life.

∾

Next day, I pay a visit to the Meishin bookshop by myself. I didn't tell Yoriko I was coming here, though she might have discovered by now since I took two pomelos with me.

Chie is in a corner arranging books. When I call out to her, she smiles at me and says, "You've been here a lot lately!"

"Did you make this too, Chie?" I ask about the POP display next to her. Beside a stack of paperbacks is a bright pink sign decorated with a border of leaves that surrounds the title *The Pink Plane Tree*, the words standing out in relief.

"Yes. *The Pink Plane Tree* by Mizue Kanata. It's just been announced that it will be made into a movie."

I notice the belly band across the cover shows a photo of two popular actresses whom I assume will star in the movie.

"It's a brilliant novel," Chie says dreamily. "The dialogue is so powerful. I get women, and men your age too, Dad, telling me they've been moved to tears by it. I'm so glad it was published in book form after the serial. It means many more people will get to read it now."

I look at her, speaking with such passion.

"Did you come here to buy a book?" she asks.

"No, I... I just wanted to ask you something."

She comes closer and whispers, "It's almost time for my break. Wait just a bit longer and then we can have lunch together."

~

Chie has forty-five minutes for lunch. She takes off her apron and we head for the restaurant section of the station building to find a soba noodle restaurant. Sitting opposite me, she takes a sip of hot-roasted green tea and breathes out a deep sigh of relief.

"Are you busy?"

"Today's not so bad."

I notice her fingernails wrapped around the mug of tea are trimmed short. When she was in college she used to grow them long and decorate them in all different colors.

Chie smiles weakly. "The subject of becoming permanent came up again but went nowhere in the end."

This year, she will have been with the company for five years, but I have heard that it is difficult to transition from contract employee to permanent status. The bookshop industry is a tough market to be in.

"I'm sorry to hear that," I tell her.

"Yeah, well, I'm just grateful to have a job."

Our order arrives. Chie is having tempura soba while I have a bowl of udon noodles with seasoned deep-fried tofu.

"I hear books aren't selling as well any more, and bookshops are disappearing," I say conversationally, holding the tofu under the broth with my chopsticks to soak up the flavors.

Chie's face clouds over. "Stop it. When everybody says that as if they know what they're talking about, it turns into a trend. Books will always be essential for some people. And bookshops are a place for those people to discover the books that will become important to them. I will never allow bookshops to vanish from this world," she finishes, noisily sucking up a mouthful of soba.

Ahhh, I hadn't realized how deeply she feels how

about her work. Nor how all this time when she's been telling me about her struggles to become permanent, she has actually been thinking in such an expansive way about the industry as a whole. Maybe this is what it means to be truly moved by one's work.

I put down my chopsticks. "I'm sorry, Chie, when you're doing your best. You're far better than me."

She shakes her head. "But Dad, you worked for the same company all your life, to the end of your career. That's really something to be proud of. You did your best. Everybody loves Honeydome cookies from Kuremiyado."

I remember Ms. Komachi said something similar.

"But I didn't make them," I reply, picking up my chopsticks again.

Chie frowns. "If that's how you think of it, then I have to say I've never sold a book that I wrote myself. But if I can sell a book that I think is good, then I'm happy. That's why I'm really into the POP displays. Because the books I recommend feel a little bit like my own." She takes a bite of tempura. "It isn't enough just to have one person writing something. Other people need to be involved. Someone has to put the word out, and someone else is the intermediary with the public. Do you know how many people are involved from the time a manuscript is written until it reaches the reader? I'm proud to be a part of that process."

Chie and I have never discussed work face-to-face like this before. When did she become so grown up?

I didn't make the Honeydome cookies. But like Chie, I believed in them passionately and worked hard to promote them. I was part of the whole process leading up to the moment when somebody puts one in their mouth and smiles with pleasure. This thought makes those forty-two years seem worthwhile.

"Oh, I just remembered," Chie says as she finishes her noodles and reaches into her tote bag. She takes out a book: *Genge and Frogs*.

"I love that you're reading Shinpei Kusano, so I bought it." She opens the book and flips through the pages. "I really like this 'Window' poem. I think it's a little different from the rest of the collection."

It makes me happy to know that the same poem has captured her attention as well as mine. "Why is it called 'Window'?" I ask. "That puzzled me."

"Hmm," Chie responds, looking down at the page. "I can picture him staying at a guesthouse, where he opens the window, and then, da-dah, there it is—the sea! Perhaps it makes a deep impression on him? Or maybe up to that moment he had only seen inside the room, so when he opens the window it is like suddenly discovering a whole wide world outside. He stands there with a breeze blowing over him, and his life converges with the vastness of the sea."

By the end of this speech, Chie is holding the book open to her chest and speaking as if carried away in her imagination. She sees a surprisingly different picture to the one I took from the same sentences. Chie's version of Shinpei Kusano is far more cheerful and positive.

In my heart I applaud the wonder of poetry. Only Shinpei Kusano knows what he actually saw. Yet each reader can have their own interpretation, which is a good thing.

Chie carefully closes the volume and affectionately pats a frog on the cover. "When I buy a book, I also become part of the process as a reader. People working in the book industry are not the only ones who make the publishing world go round; most of all it depends on the readers. Books belong to everybody: the creators, the sellers and the readers. That's what society is all about I believe."

Society. Hearing the word from Chie makes me sit up. Is she implying that people with jobs are not the only ones who make society function?

When Chie returns the book to her bag, I exclaim at the sight of the crab attached to it. She holds it up to show me with an angelic expression. "It's so cute. I put a safety pin on the back so I can use it as a pin or brooch. This works well, don't you think?"

It delights me to hear this, and I'm sure the crab would think so too. It will have a much happier life with Chie than with me.

She looks at the crab with a wistful smile. "Do you remember doing the crab race together when I was in elementary school?"

"The crab race?" I ask.

She laughs. "You don't remember? At sports day when I was in grade three. It was a race for parents and children, walking back to back in a crab walk. We came in last."

"That's right, we did, didn't we."

"You told me how unique it was to walk like a crab because the scenery goes by sideways and the world looks bigger than normal. Walking sideways gives you a wider view."

I do vaguely remember saying something like that. If that's how Chie remembers it, I have no doubt she's correct.

She looks down shyly. "You told me that if you only ever look in front, your view will be quite narrow. So whenever I feel stuck or don't know what to do, I try to broaden my view. Relax my shoulders and walk sideways like a crab."

A lump forms in my throat and I have to try to stop the tears. For so long I have worried about Chie. Worried that she has no memories of spending time with me because I had left all the childcare up to Yoriko. I worried that I had not been able to teach my daughter anything.

Now I think I finally understand what Mr. Ebigawa was saying. Whenever people interact, that is being part of society. And the things that happen as a result of those points of contact exist in the past and the future.

The company is not everything. Parents and children are a "society" too. Chie had taken the words that I uttered to her so casually when she was small, and made them her own. It touches me deeply to see her now, so mature and grown-up.

The crab attached to Chie's bag looks at me, as if it is going to move.

For so long now I have been trying to walk forward, and only forward. Believing that life is a linear journey that stretches straight ahead of us. If I look sideways now, what will I see? How will my daily life, my wife and daughter appear to me?

Chie raises her hand to attract the waiter's attention and asks for another cup of roasted green tea. Then she says, "By the way, what did you want to ask me?"

～

A few days later, I arrive at the Community House library late in the afternoon to return my books. The young man in the green shirt from the other day is attaching a poster to the bulletin board that partitions off the reference corner. Nozomi is giving him instructions from a short distance away.

"Hiroya, move it up a bit more and to the right."

Hiroya removes a drawing pin from the top right-hand corner and adjusts the position. The poster, an advertisement for "Librarian for a Day," has an eye-catching, mysterious illustration on it: a sheep with spiral horns so ornate they almost have a personality of their own is holding an open book.

"Hello," I say as I walk by.

Nozomi smiles at me and says, "Oh, hello," in return.

On the other side of the screen, sure enough, I find Ms. Komachi plying her needle. She stops when she notices me, and her gaze shifts to the paper bag in my hands with the Kuremiyado logo on it.

"I brought you some supplies," I say, taking the box out of the paper bag. Inside are twelve Honeydome cookies.

Putting both hands to her cheeks, she looks at the box and gives a contented sigh.

In my heart I have accepted now that these are "my" Honeydomes, and plan to continue championing them, confidently and with pride, and of course eat them too.

Ms. Komachi stands to accept the box. "Thank you very much."

"Last time you asked me about what to call the last two Honeydomes remaining in a box of twelve. Well, I think I know the answer to that question now."

She looks at me expectantly, with the box still in her hands.

"The last two in the box are no different from the first Honeydome cookie one eats. Every Honeydome is as good as all the others."

I know that now. Just as every day is equal in value and no less important than all the others. The day I was born, today as I stand here now and the many tomorrows to come.

Ms. Komachi gives a big smile of satisfaction and sits down with the box in her arms.

"May I ask something?" I say.

"What is it?"

"About the bonus gifts… How do you choose them?"

When it comes to books, I am sure Ms. Komachi draws on her intuition and many years of experience as a librarian to decide which books would suit different readers. However, she could not have known I would come across river crabs in the supermarket, or my experience with crab-walking at the school sports day. She must have some special power, I feel sure of it.

"I just choose at random," she answers.

"I beg your pardon?"

"Well, if you want to put a name to it, inspiration."

"Inspiration?"

"If my choice happened to strike a chord with you, I'm delighted to hear it." She looks me straight in the eye. "But you have to understand that even if I have some inkling about a person, I don't tell them anything. People find meaning in the bonus gifts for themselves. It's the same with books. Readers make their own personal connections to words, irrespective of the writer's intentions, and each reader gains something unique."

Ms. Komachi holds up the box. "Thank you very much for this. I will share it with my husband."

I picture Mr. and Mrs. Komachi with the box of Honeydomes open between them, the soft-centered cookies bringing joy to their eyes, tongues and hearts. I am proud to be part of the chain that brought them this.

～

On a sunny afternoon I meet Yoriko in the lobby of a community center. She has been teaching a computer class for seniors during the morning, and we are going to have a picnic afterward.

We stroll together through the park where the cherry trees are now a leafy green. In my backpack I carry rice balls as a surprise for her. Recently, I have been practising making them in secret whenever she goes out, and I know from having asked Chie during our lunch at the soba shop that Yoriko's favorite rice ball filling is pickled nozawana leafy greens. I am glad I asked, as I would never have guessed that on my own. To think that all this time I didn't even know that, while Yoriko knows exactly what my tastes are.

We sit down on the bench and I pull out the rice balls covered in plastic wrap. Yoriko cries out in surprise and looks from my face to the rice ball, and back again, before taking a bite.

"Mmm, it's nozawana!" she exclaims happily. Seeing her so happy makes me happy, too.

She looks down in her lap and says, "Masao, do you remember when I lost my job and you took me for a drive to Nagano?"

"Er, yes, I do."

Yoriko was forty when she was fired. The company she worked for got into financial difficulties and she was among the first to be dismissed. The assumption was that it would be okay to fire her because she had a husband to support her.

At the time she had cried in frustration, "This has nothing to do with my actual ability."

I didn't know what to say, as I'm so bad at talking, so

I simply offered to take her for a drive. I thought a day trip to a hot spring might be a good distraction.

Still looking at the rice ball in her hand, Yoriko continues. "I remember sitting in the passenger seat, looking at you and feeling devastated because I'd been fired, when in fact I hadn't lost anything. I myself was no different than before. I'd simply left the company I worked for. That's all. I still had the option to derive joy from my work and happiness from spending time with my loved ones. It all just depended on me, and what I did from then on. That's when I realized that I wanted to work freelance in future."

She turns toward me with a smile. "The nozawana I ate in Nagano that day was so delicious it's been my favorite in rice balls ever since."

I return the smile. I had cheated by getting the tip about nozawana from Chie, but I'll let myself off the hook and not confess to it.

I will not forget this day either. The two of us, sitting side by side, eating rice balls in the park. I remove the wrapping from my own rice ball and start eating.

"Mr. Yakita was delighted you came. Is the class interesting?" Yoriko asks.

I have already paid this month's fee for the Go class. And reread the introductory book on Go that Ms. Komachi recommended to me. The sense of familiarity I felt as I read it, despite not knowing the game, came I am sure from actually having touched Go stones in class that one time. Without this experience I doubt if I would have felt the same. It's amazing what a difference doing something just once can make. I have an urge now to know more about the kinds of drama that might be revealed by Go.

"It's difficult," I tell her. "No matter how hard I try to remember I forget." I laugh. "But I don't mind, because I enjoy finding things out over and over again. I'll stick with it for a while."

Until now, I have always thought of things in terms of whether or not they could be useful to me in some way. But that may have become my stumbling block. Now I know the importance of the heart being moved, I have a list of things I want to try. Learning to make buckwheat soba noodles, for one, and tour historical sites and do English conversation lessons online, on the computer that Yoriko taught me how to use. I'd even like to try wool felting. And if I happen to see any job vacancy posting that moves me, then I might give that a try too.

My plan is to appreciate every new day. And take a wide view of things.

After we finish eating, Yoriko and I walk through the early summer greenery in the park, me in my sneakers, of course. Birds sing. A breeze blows. Yoriko walks beside me smiling. I will not give up on myself. From now on, I intend to gather close all the things that are important to me. I will make my own anthology.

Words bubble up in my head and spill from my lips spontaneously.

Maa-maa-maa-maa,
Masao moves along.
Sah-sah-sah-sah,
Masao is looking strong.
Oh-oh-oh-oh,
With Yoriko by his side.

Yoriko looks startled. "What's that?"

"It's 'Masao's Song.'"

"Hmm, not bad," says Yoriko with a nod.

★ ★ ★ ★ ★

Details of the books mentioned in
What You Are Looking For Is in the Library

『ぐりとぐら』 中川李枝子 文 大村百合子 絵 福音
館書店
Guri and Gura, by Rieko Nakagawa and illustrated by
Yuriko Ohmura—a well-known Japanese children's picture book published by Fukuinkan Shoten.

『英国王立園芸協会とたのしむ 植物のふしぎ』 ガイ・
バーター著 北綾子訳 河出書房新社
*How Do Worms Work? A Gardener's Collection of Curi-
ous Questions and Astonishing Answers* by Guy Barter, a
title from the British Royal Horticultural Society about
the wonder of plants, published by KAWADE SHOBO
SHINSHA.

『月のとびら』『新装版　月のとびら』　石井ゆかり著
阪急コミュニケーションズ/ CCCメディアハウス
Moon Petals by Yukari Ishii—a Japanese book about astrology, first edition published by Hankyu Communications, new edition published by CCC Media House.

『ビジュアル　進化の記録　ダーウィンたちの見た世界』
デビッド・クアメン　ジョセフ・ウォレス著　渡辺政隆監訳
ポプラ社
Evolution: A Visual Record by Robert Clark and Joseph Wallace—a book of photographs of the natural world, published by POPLAR.

『げんげと蛙』草野心平著　銀の鈴社
Genge and Frogs by Shinpei Kusano—a twentieth-century Japanese poetry collection, published by Gin-no-Suzu.

『21エモン』　藤子・F・不二雄著　小学館
21 Emon, text and illustrations by Fujiko F. Fujio, published by Shogakukan. Japanese manga.

『らんま1/2』『うる星やつら』『めぞん一刻』高橋留美子著　小学館
Ranma ½, Urusei Yatsura, Maison Ikkoku, text and illustrations by Rumiko Takahashi, published by Shogakukan. Three Japanese manga stories.

『漂流教室』　楳図かずお著　小学館
The Drifting Classroom, text and illustrations by Kazuo Umezu, published by Shogakukan. Japanese horror manga.

『MASTERキートン』　浦沢直樹著　小学館
Master Keaton, text and illustrations by Naoki Urasawa, published by Shogakukan. Japanese manga.

『日出処の天子』　山岸涼子著　白泉社
Emperor of the Land of the Rising Sun, text and illustrations by Ryoko Yamagishi, published by Hakusensha. Japanese manga.

『北斗の拳』　武論尊原作　原哲夫作画　集英社
Fist of the North Star, text by Buronson and illustrations by Tetsuo Hara, published by SHUEISHA. Japanese manga.

『火の鳥』手塚治虫著 KADOKAWA

Phoenix, Bird of Fire, text and illustrations by Osamu Tezuka,
published by KADOKAWA. Japanese manga.